My
Name
Is
~~Brain~~
BRIAN

Other Apple Paperbacks
you will enjoy:

My Name Is ~~Brain~~ BRIAN

JEANNE BETANCOURT

SCHOLASTIC INC.
New York Toronto London Auckland Sydney
Mexico City New Delhi Hong Kong Buenos Aires

ISBN-13: 978-0-590-44922-9
ISBN-10: 0-590-44922-2

29   16 17 18 19 20
                    Printed in the U.S.A.   40

For Nicole Marie Betancourt

Contents

Acknowledgments

I am very grateful to Theresa Collins, Diana King, and Shirley Kokesh for their diligent and creative consulting.

Thank-you also goes to Christine Kilmer, Karl Oppenheimer, and their students at Kildonan School, particularly John Dean, Chris Murphy, Chris Rutan, and Ryan Thuman; to Iris Spano at the New York Branch of the Orton Society; to Joann Chandler from the Northeast Audubon Center; to Mike Dudek at the Miles Wildlife Sanctuary; and to Paul Feder, Nola Thacker, and Jean Feiwel. They have all offered many valuable suggestions in the development of Brian's story.

My
Name
Is
~~Brain~~
BRIAN

1

The Jokers Club

School starts tomorrow.

I hate school.

I look around the Jokers Club's hideout and wish like crazy that it was the first day of summer vacation again.

"Today vacation is officially over for the Jokers Club," I tell my fellow club members — Dan, Richie, and John.

"But we'll still meet here," Dan says, "on weekends and after school sometimes."

"Yeah," I say, "but it won't be the same. School's no fun. It's boring."

"Yeah," Richie says, "the pits."

Our hideout is the gardener's shed behind the old Colgate mansion. No one has lived in the mansion for years. Probably because it's run-down and too big for your normal sort of family. One rainy day we snuck into the main house through a cellar window and walked around the whole place counting rooms. If you include bathrooms, there are twenty-seven rooms. My grandpa Al says that when he was a kid, the Colgates were the richest people in the whole county.

But the gardener's shed — our hideout — is your basic one-room, one-window, no-bathroom shed. Rusty tools, like rakes and shovels, hang on one wall. A long, wooden worktable stands along the facing wall. Under the table there's a wheelbarrow and stacks of old clay pots. We hide our sodas and junk food in the pots, because you never know when a real estate person might come to the shed to show it to a client. I don't think anyone who's buying a twenty-seven-room house will care what the inside of the shed looks like, but you never know.

"Hey, I've got a great idea," John says. "Let's not go to school tomorrow. We'll meet here instead, like usual."

"Sure," Richie agrees. "Why not?"

"Because I can't," I tell them. "I gotta go to school. My parents would kill me."

My parents are the strictest.

Dan's are the next strictest.

Richie's come next. But his mother works late at the supermarket, so sometimes it doesn't make any difference when he gets home.

John's parents try to be strict, but he does pretty much what he wants, no matter what they say. Once I heard John yell and swear at his mother.

Now John's telling us, "You guys are wimps. Gutless wonders. Nerdballs." Then he flashes his big "just kidding" smile. "Okay," he says, "if we've got to go to school, let's think of something we can do to make it more fun — besides teasing girls and not doing any work."

I'm feeling too depressed about school starting to have any fun ideas about anything. So I just sit there thinking about my friends and waiting for one of them to come up with an idea.

John's stretched out on the long worktable. He's the biggest, baddest, and oldest in our club. He's already twelve. He's the strongest, too.

Dan's spot in the hideout is near the door in an easy chair he made out of two bags of sand. Dan's the smallest of the Jokers and the nicest — according to me. He also has the darkest skin of anyone in Sharon, Connecticut, population 2,545. Both his mother and father are African-American. There are only three black kids in our school, and Dan is one of them. The other two are his brother and sister. Dan's family moved to Sharon last year.

Dan's leaning back in his sandbag chair, looking at the slanted roof of the hideout, thinking. Probably about monsters. Dan loves monster movies, even when they scare him half to death. If it's just the two of us watching, I cover my eyes during the worst parts and say, "Tell me when it's over." But he can watch the whole thing. He also loves to draw

3

and has about a hundred drawings of freaky-looking monster characters.

Richie, our fourth Joker, sits on a wooden stool. He's a redhead and the skinniest and fastest of my friends. Nobody I know can beat Richie in a race, not even John. Any kind of race. Even stupid races, like "Put the handle of a spoon in your mouth, balance a raw egg on the spoon part, and walk across the schoolyard." Richie always wins.

Me? I'm Brian Toomey. And I'm your in-between kind of kid. I'm in between John and Dan height-wise. I'm in between Richie and John sports-wise. My mom says I'm the best-looking boy she knows. But my sister, Hilary, says I'm the ugliest thing that's ever walked the face of the earth. So I guess maybe I'm in between in the good looks department, too.

My position in the hideout is on top of two bales of hay that are stacked under the window. I'm the lookout who warns the others if someone is coming. Sometimes I hear a noise and signal an alert for everyone to get ready to sneak out. But when I look real hard, I can see the noise is from a deer or a raccoon or some other four-legged animal.

John sits up. "So who's got an idea?" he says. "If we can't think of something to make school more fun, I'm not going." I wonder what John would do if he didn't go to school. He couldn't come to the hideout alone. That's the first rule of the Jokers Club:

"No one goes to the hideout unless everyone comes." When Richie visited his cousin in Ohio at the beginning of August, none of us went for a whole week.

"Maybe if we had a secret game or something," Richie suggests.

John makes a fist and punches the air. "I got it," he says. "We're great jokers, right? Always being funny . . . ?"

"We try," I say.

"Here's what we do. We do funny things in school."

"But we do that anyway," I remind him. "That's what we do. We're the Jokers Club."

"But we've never kept score before," John says.

In the next half hour we come up with a brilliant plan on how the Jokers Club will work during the school year. I name it Operation J.D.B.R. Besides those letters being the initials of our first names — John, Dan, Brian, Richie — the letters also stand for "A Joke a Day Brings Relief."

We decide that the Joker who makes a joke in school that makes people laugh the most wins points for the day.

Here's how the scoring goes: 2 points for the joke of the day; 1 bonus point if the joke is on a girl, but 2 bonus points if the joke is on the girl we hate the most — Isabel Morris.

There are three rules.

1. No jokes like, "Why did the chicken cross the road?" or "Why did the elephant do such and such?" Only real, original practical jokes.

2. No jokes on members of the Jokers Club.

3. Scratch your head if you think a joke is the joke of the day for Operation J.D.B.R.

"An example of a real good joke," John says, "is making a handfart when Ms. Olgey leans over." We all like that.

"Do we get a girl bonus point since the joke's on her?" Richie asks.

"Sure," John tells him. "She's not a guy, is she?"

Everyone at Sharon Center School knows that the sixth-grade teacher, Ms. Olgey, is a pushover. The principal always has to go into her classroom to get the kids to quiet down.

"So what's the prize," Richie asks, "for getting the most points?"

"Money!" John says. "Let's make a pot of money, a stash of cash, and divvy it up at the end by how many points we have."

"How?" I ask.

Dan says that if we divide the amount of money we collect by the total number of points we've won, it'll tell us how much each point is worth. He explains his idea with an example. "If there's two hundred dollars in the pot, and we've won a total of fifty points, then each point is worth four dollars."

John and Richie look confused, but I get it right away. "So if a point is worth four dollars," I say, "and I have ten points, then I make ten points times four dollars, which equals forty dollars."

After a few more examples, we all understand and agree to each contribute two dollars a week to the pot and to divide it during Christmas vacation when, according to Dan, it will be worth $120. We elect Dan as scorekeeper, and John as treasurer.

"Maybe going to school won't be so bad after all," John says as we drag our bikes from their hiding places behind the bushes. We put on our helmets and silently bike through the woods to Route 343. As the lookout, I wait until there are no cars coming in either direction before signaling to the others that it's all-clear.

Then the Jokers roll onto the highway and pedal toward town, chanting out the initials of our new operation. "J.D.B.R., J.D.B.R., J.D.B.R."

2

Brian: 2 Points

That night I have a terrible nightmare.

An army of huge gray rocks — each as tall as a refrigerator — are chasing me. I'm screaming for help as I try to run away from them. I'm out of breath. The monster rocks are falling toward me. They are going to bury me. I'll be crushed to death. I scream, but no sounds come out. . . .

I wake up.

I open my eyes and look around frantically. There are no big, oddly shaped gray rocks, just my attic bedroom with its slanty ceiling. I'm sweating and breathing hard, as if I'd really been running.

I've had this nightmare before.

I get out of bed and head down to the bathroom thinking about how my nightmare is like a monster movie. I decide to ride my bike over to Dan's house after breakfast and tell him that I'm going to quit renting monster movies with him. Then I remember that Dan and I won't be watching any movies today, or cruising around on our bikes, or hanging out with John and Richie at the hideout. I remember that summer is over.

So does my mother, who yells up the staircase, "First day of school, Brian. Put a move on."

School. I hate it.

I open the bathroom door.

"Hey! I'm in here," my sister, Hilary, yells. She's standing at the bathroom mirror putting on lipstick.

"Hurry up," I tell her. I scrunch up my nose and sniff. "Phew. You smell like a perfume factory."

"It's better than smelling like your breath," she says as she pushes by me. "That smells like old garbage."

"Oh, yeah. YOUR breath smells like . . ." Before I can think of something worse than garbage, she says, "Just kidding. How do I look?"

I check her out. Same brownish hair pulled back in a ponytail. Same five feet two inches tall. Same crooked smile showing a mouthful of braces. Something is printed across her royal-blue sweatshirt in yellow letters. I guess it's the name of our high school, Housatonic Regional High.

"You look like usual," I tell her. "Nice shirt."

She grunts a thanks and reminds me that now she's in high school she'll be taking the school bus, while I'll still have to bike or walk to Sharon Center School.

When I come into the kitchen a few minutes later,

my little brother, Tyson, starts up his morning chant of "Brian, Brian, Brian." I sit in my regular chair next to his high chair and give him a high five, low five, slide five, and shake out some cereal for myself. Tyson is the person I get along with best in our family. Hilary says that's because he's two-and-a-half years old and I have the mind of a two-year-old.

"Brian," my mom says, "it's almost eight o'clock. You'll have to start getting up earlier. No notes from school this year about lateness. Where are your new school supplies?"

"Upstairs," I say through a slurp of milky cereal.

"Don't answer with food in your mouth," she scolds.

My father's at the counter rolling up architectural plans for an addition he's building on somebody's house. "Brian, I don't want to be called up to that school this year," he scolds. "Do you understand?" He walks over and glares down at me. I continue eating my cereal while he lectures. "No more goofing off. I want to see some hard work out of you this year." He taps me on the head with his roll of plans. "I want to see results. The day I have to go to that school is the day you say good-bye to your karate lessons."

Tyson pulls on my sleeve. "Do karate. Do karate."

"Now I'm late," my dad grumbles to my mom as he picks up his lunch pail and heads out the back door. He says it like it's my fault.

As I get up from the table I do a front snap kick. Tyson claps happily and chants, "Karate. Karate." So I do another kick. Unfortunately, this one hits the leg of Hilary's chair just as she's stuffing a spoonful of cereal and milk into her mouth.

"Mom!" my sister screams, "look what Brian did." White milk drips down the front of her bright blue sweatshirt. "You jerk," she yells.

"Sor-ry," I yell back as I hustle out of the room. "Gotta go."

Under my bed I find the paper bag with my new school supplies. I sit on the floor and flip through the bright red notebook. One hundred and fifty clean white pages separated into five sections by yellow dividers. I think, it's a new school year. Maybe this year I'll start out good, right from the beginning. I'll do all my homework and pay attention in class. I'm as smart as anybody else. I can do it. I just didn't try hard enough before. This year I'll try real hard, right from the beginning. A new beginning with a new teacher. Naturally I won't tell the other Jokers. I'll keep it a secret from them, but I make a vow to myself: "This year I'll really try. I can do it."

Riding my bike to school, I chant with each push of the pedal, "I can do it. I can do it."

"Hey, man, wait up." John's bike pulls up next to mine.

"How's it going?" I ask.

"Great!" he says. "I heard Ms. Olgey quit teaching. We're getting a new teacher who never taught here before. She's probably never taught anywhere. She'll be a bigger pushover than the other one. Think of some jokes. Some humdingers, man." He rears up on his back wheel to celebrate.

As we go down the hill I see the school's new shingle roof. Early last spring they replaced the old leaky roof with a new one. One day, after the crew went home, I went back to school, climbed the scaffolding to the roof, and sat up there. I could see the sun behind the mountains in New York State. Then I saw hundreds of black specks flying toward me in a perfect V-shaped formation. Canada geese, honking like crazy, as they flew north.

I wonder what it would be like to be a Canada goose. Not the lead one, just one of those riding the current near the back of the line and honking away.

All summer I've been thinking about those geese. Geese must be pretty smart to know enough to go north when it's hot in the south, and south when it's cold in the north. I decided that they must be communicating to one another with all that honking.

I wish I could go up to the roof now and wait for the geese to pass over school on their way south again. But I can't. John and I are riding our bikes into the schoolyard through a bunch of noisy kids. "Get off those bikes," a teacher's aide yells. "No riding in the yard."

Dan and Richie are waiting for us by the bike rack. The bell rings. Everyone else goes in. But we hang back, talking about how much we hate school, until the principal, Ms. Freedman, shouts, "Let's go, gentlemen." We pretend we don't hear her. None of us wants to be the first to do what she says. Ms. Freedman claps her hands and shouts impatiently, "Now."

"School," Richie says as we finally go into the building. "I hate it."

John looks around. "This place is like prison."

"Yeah," Dan agrees. "The pits."

I say, "It's the worst," but I'm thinking about how I'm going to try hard, right from the first day. I'm thinking *I can do it this time*.

A tall black man with gray hair, dressed in a dark blue suit — a man as big as any prizefighter — is standing in front of the doorway of room 106. Before I can whisper to my friends "Who's that?" he turns sharply and faces us.

"I've been waiting for you," he says in a deep growl of a voice. He gives each of us a stern look.

The four of us stop dead in our tracks. I shiver with fear because I know who he is. This man is a plainclothes cop. He knows about our hideout. He knows that we ignored the NO TRESPASSING signs hundreds of times. He knows that we broke into the Colgate mansion. He will arrest us.

He takes a step toward us, looks us each right in the eye, and says, "I'm Mr. Bigham, your sixth-grade teacher. And you gentlemen are?"

I manage to stammer, "Brian Toomey, sir."

After we've all introduced ourselves, Mr. Bigham puts out his arm to show us that we should go into the room ahead of him.

As John passes in front of Mr. Bigham, he looks up at him and says, "We can sit anywhere we want, right?"

"Wrong," Mr. Bigham answers. "There are name cards on the desks." He immediately starts giving directions to the class so we don't have time to start fooling around, even if we dared. I know that Mr. Bigham already knows that we are the troublemakers because he has our desks as far from one another as possible.

I'm stuck between Jay Preston and Isabel Morris. They were the biggest brains in fifth grade . . . and the biggest pains. My luck. I see Isabel give Jay a look that says she isn't too happy to be sitting next to me, either.

It's easy to be a good student for the first hour. All we have to do is listen to announcements over the loudspeaker and to Mr. Bigham's speech about doing good right from the beginning of the year. That's what I plan to do anyway.

Then he makes a list on the board of our suggestions for good classroom management. I don't think Mr. Bigham will have trouble managing a classroom. It's hard to imagine anyone having the courage to do a handfart when Mr. Bigham bends over.

During recess the Jokers Club has an emergency meeting by the bike rack.

"This is going to be a miserable year," Richie says. "He's scary."

"Like some kind of bionic man," Dan says. "I bet he lifts weights all the time."

"I wonder where he came from?" I ask.

"Maybe he's an ex-con," Richie says, "and every once in a while a school has to take one, for rehabilitation and stuff."

"I bet he wanted to be a football coach, and this is the only job he could get," I say.

"Which must make him very mad," Dan adds.

"How are we going to make jokes in his room?" Richie asks John. "He'll kill us."

"Operation J.D.B.R. lives," John says. "Don't let him scare you, guys. He's just another person. There's only one of him and four of us. We're not going into the boxing ring with him. And there are laws against hitting kids. If he hits one of us, we could sue him and become millionaires."

"Dead millionaires," I mumble.

The bell rings for the end of recess. We don't wait to be last, but go right in with the other kids heading back to room 106. "Remember," John whispers, "Operation J.D.B.R. lives."

Mr. Bigham is waiting for us at the door. As we pass him, he tells us to write our names on the board, last names first. It seems like a silly thing to be doing since he already has a list of our names. I print mine.

When we're back in our places he tells us to alphabetize the names written on the board. I open my notebook and look down at the clean page. I pick up my pencil and silently repeat my vow to do better this year. Then I take a deep breath and look at the board for last names that begin with "A." I copy "Andrews, Karen," on my paper. Under it I write, "Abbot, Kevin."

"Class," Mr. Bigham asks, "what do you do if there are two or more names that begin with the same letter?"

Before anyone else has a chance to think, Isabel waves her hand and says, "Look at the second letter."

I glance over at her paper. There are already at least five names neatly penned in script.

I look at my thick gray pencil marks. The second letter of Andrews is "N" and the second letter of

Abbot is "B." I recite the alphabet to myself. "B" comes before "N." I erase what I'd written.

Out of the corner of my eye I see Isabel. With one hand she's covering her mouth to hold back a laugh. With the other hand she's trying to get Jay's attention. When he looks up, she points at me. Jay looks at the board, then at me, and giggles.

"Is something wrong, Jason?" Mr. Bigham asks.

"It's Brian," Jay answers shyly. "Look how he wrote his name."

Mr. Bigham and everyone else in the room looks at the board. I read, "Toomey, Brian." What's the big deal?

"I'm not the only one who printed," I call out.

Other people in the room start laughing. Not your big laugh, but one of those quiet little laughs you would use if you had a teacher who looked like a kid-crunching machine.

John points at the board. "Brain?" he chortles. "Brian, you're a riot, man. 'Brian the Brain.' I love it." He scratches his head. So do Richie and Dan. I've made a joke without even trying. I don't even know what the joke is.

Mr. Bigham's actually smiling as he goes up to the board. "Very funny, Brian," he says. "Let's just fix it."

Just before Mr. Bigham erases my name, I see my

mistake. "B-r-a-i-n." I wrote "Brain" instead of "Brian."

"He didn't do it to be funny," Isabel calls out. "It was a mistake." Some kids laugh a little louder.

"It was a joke," I lie.

"Sure," Isabel mumbles under her breath.

Mr. Bigham turns from the board and looks around. "Enough," is all he says. The room becomes so quiet, you could have heard a kid's bone break.

"This is a timed assignment," Mr. Bigham announces. "Ten more minutes."

I look down at my paper. How can I do well in school if I can't even spell my own name right? I look through the list on the board for a name that begins with "B," then "C," while Mr. Bigham walks around the room checking the work. When he reaches my desk, he leans over and whispers, "Brian, alphabetize by last names, not first names."

I look at my paper. I've written "Ann. Brad. Charlene."

Isabel covers her mouth so Mr. Bigham won't see that she's laughing at me again. I hate Isabel.

I try to erase the big gray letters. Why did I press down so hard when I wrote? Now I'll never get them off. Big gray letters. Big gray rocks. Being chased by huge rocks. My nightmare comes back, and I realize that the rock-monsters were shaped like the letters of the alphabet. They *were* the alphabet. Big stone alphabet letters crushing me to death. I think about how much I hate the letters of the alphabet and press down even harder on my eraser. My paper rips.

"Time," Mr. Bigham calls out. "Pass your papers forward."

3

Brian: 2 Points
+ 1 Big Point
+ 2 Isabel Points

By Thursday of the first week of school I'm the only one who has any points that were won in Mr. Bigham's class. During Mr. Dithers' social studies class, John scored by making a chain out of Dithers' pile of paper clips. Dithers didn't figure out that all of his clips were linked until he'd taken off three of them. By then everyone in the room was cracking up. Richie scored in Mr. Firestone's gym class by planting a big blob of plastic blood on the gym floor. Before he realized it was fake, Firestone gave a frightened sweeping look around the gym like the next thing he expected to see was a dead body under the bleachers.

But getting points in Mr. Bigham's classes — math, English, science, and homeroom — is the big challenge. So from now on if Mr. Bigham is in the room when you score, we call the joke a Big Joke, and it's worth an extra point called a Big Point. John and Richie had both tried Big Jokes, but no one in the class dared laugh, so they didn't score.

I've given up my idea about new beginnings and fresh starts. It's hopeless. I'm hopeless. I'm in the lowest reading group, and in math I can't remember the multiplication tables, even easy ones like the five-times tables. In social studies we're studying states and their capitals and what each state is famous for — like maple syrup from Vermont. I can't remember any of them but that one. I live for recess, lunch hour, and journal-writing period.

For a person who hates school, to like journal-writing period may sound weird. The reason I like journal writing is because we don't have to write anything if we don't want to, so I don't. The only rule is you have to be holding a pencil and have your journal book open. So for ten minutes a day I can daydream without anyone saying, "Stop day-dreaming," or asking me the answer to something I don't know. The only noise in the room is the scraping of pencils and the hushed voices of Mr. Bigham talking with one kid at a time. It's nice.

John and Dan and Richie say they aren't writing anything in their journals, either, though it looks like Dan is doing something. I figure he's drawing monsters. I hope he's smart enough not to do one that looks like Mr. Bigham.

One thing I think about a lot during journal time

is those Canada geese. I figure they'll be coming back through Sharon on their way south. I think about where I can go to watch for them. This time I want to be higher up than the roof of Sharon Center School, which is only one-story high.

During English Mr. Bigham passes out copies of the play *West Side Story*. After he talks about it, he assigns parts for reading the first scene out loud. "Brian," he says, "you read Carlos's part. He comes in on page six." I glance at the clock. With any luck, the bell will ring before we get to my part. I half listen to Isabel reading Maria's lines, and Jay reading Tony's. I turn the pages when everyone else does. Suddenly, Isabel is hissing, "It's your turn," and pointing to the top of page six.

I take a deep breath and begin. Everyone else has read fast and smart. But not me. I'm slow and stupid. Mr. Bigham or Isabel have to tell me half the words. A couple of kids groan. Finally my part is over, and it's Isabel's turn again. She reads so fast that Mr. Bigham says, "Isabel, read that speech again. Slower, please, and with more expression."

I look at the clock. When all three hands reach twelve, it'll be lunchtime. I stop listening to the play and pretend I'm counting down a shuttle lift-off. Ten. Nine. Eight. Seven. Six. Five. Four. Three. Two. One. The bell rings, and it's lift-off for me. I jump out of my chair . . . and trip over Isabel's foot. SLAM. I'm on the floor, face down.

22

Before I can get up, Mr. Bigham's standing over me. "What happened here, Brian?"

I point to Isabel as I get back on my feet and say, "I fell for her."

Everyone laughs, even Mr. Bigham. John, Dan, and Richie scratch their heads like crazy.

I stammer, "I mean I fell OVER her. She tripped me."

"I did not," Isabel says. "You got up before the bell rang."

"That's a total lie," I say.

Mr. Bigham does a low, slow "enough," and everyone quiets down. "Now, class," he says, "you may be excused for lunch."

I'm following the others to the door when Mr. Bigham stops me with his big hand. "Wait a minute, Brian. I want to speak to you."

"But — she — tripped me," I stammer.

"This has nothing to do with you and Isabel," he says. Me and Isabel? I can't believe he put us in the same breath. Then he tells me that as soon as I eat lunch, I should meet him in a conference room in the library to take a special test. "It's to see what areas you're having difficulty in," he says. "I want to help you."

Sure, I think, help me find out how retarded I am.

After lunch I go to the conference room. Mr. Bigham is already there.

During the first part of the test, he asks me questions that I answer by talking. A lot of those questions are easy and after a while, it's sort of fun.

"Excellent," he says.

"That's very good," he says.

Then he tells me to read some questions myself and write the answers. "Take as much time as you need," he says. "Get up and stretch if you get tired. You're excused from your next class." He stands up himself. "I'll be back in a little while to see how you're doing."

After finishing the first set of questions, I go over to the library window and look out at the other kids playing soccer. Richie misses a ball I know I could have gotten. Jenny makes a strong kick. The girls who play soccer with us — Jenny, Irene, and Mary — are as good as we are. But the snotty-acting girls — the ones who wear dangling earrings and wild-colored clothes and already go to the seventh-grade parties — don't play at all. They just hang out watching and giggling.

I see Isabel, sitting on the ground with her back against the building and her face in a book. Isabel isn't playing with anyone. She never does. She's not even popular with the *un*popular girls. All Isabel cares about is being smarter than anyone and showing it off. She's also weird-looking — bigger than anyone else in sixth grade, even John. And she has this long black hair that's always hanging in her face and looking like it's full of cooties. John calls her

24

"ape." The only time Isabel smiles is when she gives the right answer to a question in class or when someone else gives the wrong answer.

The bell rings for the end of lunch and I go back to the test.

Friday, as we're leaving for the day, Mr. Bigham stops me again. This time he hands me an envelope. "Brian, give your parents this note. I'm setting up a meeting with them for next week."

"I didn't do anything wrong," I tell him. "Isabel and Jay bother me all the time. Maybe you should move me."

"I want to speak to your parents about your academic work, Brian," he explains, "not your classroom behavior." I think about how little work I've done in school. Of my broken vow to do better. Of the homework I didn't finish. Of not writing in my journal. I remember my father's threat: "The day I have to go to that school is the day you say goodbye to your karate lessons."

Because I'm more afraid of my father than I am of Mr. Bigham, I blurt out, "You said we don't have to write in our journals if we don't want to. I hold my pencil the whole time."

"Brian, you are having difficulty with your schoolwork, but you're a very bright young man. I want to help you. I want us all to help you. That means I need to see your parents."

"They never come to school." I try to hand him back the envelope. "It's a rule in our house. They never come. I'll do better work. I promise." I pat my backpack. "Look. I got all my homework."

He hands the envelope back to me. "Give it to them, Brian. My home phone number is on it. If there's a problem about coming to school, let them tell me themselves."

"Freedom. Freedom," John shouts as we bike-race one another to the hideout after school.

It's a sunny, hot, summerlike day. We hide our bikes in the woods and go in through the door of the shed. I take a deep breath of musty air. Boy, it feels good to be back.

As soon as we're in our places, Dan takes out the little notebook he's using for Operation J.D.B.R. scores, and recites, "Brian, seven points for jokes on Monday and Thursday; John, two points for a joke on Tuesday; Richie, two for a joke on Wednesday; Dan, zero. Nobody scored today."

We each give John two dollars for the pot. Dan says that since we have eight dollars and we've earned a total of eleven points, each point is worth $.72.

"How do you figure that?" Richie asks.

"I divided the value of the pot by the number of points," Dan explains. "Eight dollars divided by eleven points equals $.7272$, which I rounded off to to $.72$. So, if we divided the pot today, I'd get zero times $.72$, which equals zilch. Richie and John, you'd each get two times $.72$, which equals 1.44, and Brian would be the winner with seven times $.72$ or 5.04. There'd be one cent left over," he adds, "which we could just leave in the pot."

No one says how amazing it is that Dan figured this out. John grabs me in the arm lock and says, "Good thing we're not dividing it until Christmas. Gives me plenty of time to catch up." I back kick him, and we fool around like that while Dan and Richie look for a safe place to keep the money. They find an old tobacco can filled with nails. We empty out the nails, put the money in the can, and hide it in the crawl space under the shed.

Richie gets the last of our summer supply of candy out of a clay planter. "Let's each have a chocolate bar. Whaddaya say?"

We all cheer. "And let's pretend this is the first weekend of summer vacation," Dan says. "Let's pretend it all weekend."

"Yeah," John agrees as he catches the candy that Richie throws in his direction.

As I catch my candy bar, John says, "Brian, you were a riot. First, 'Brian the Brain.' And then to say, 'I fell for Isabel.' Man, that was brilliant."

While they're all congratulating me, I'm thinking I didn't make either of the jokes on purpose, and I don't even think they're very funny. I also remember the note from Mr. Bigham in my backpack and don't feel brilliant or like celebrating. This weekend is going to be the beginning of the end of my life . . . and of my karate lessons.

4

Brian: 2 Points + 1 Big Point

I wait until after my karate class on Saturday to give my mother the note from Mr. Bigham. "Your father is going to have a fit," she says when she's read it. "But I can't begin to deal with this now. Go take care of your brother while I make dinner."

I'm in the living room showing Tyson my new karate move — an uppercut punch to the jaw — when I hear my dad's pickup rumble into our driveway. A few minutes later he's shaking the note from Mr. Bigham in my face and screaming at me. "Just look at this. You've been in school one week and you're already in trouble."

"But I didn't do anything," I tell him.

"Exactly what I was afraid of," he yells. "You didn't do anything. Let me see your notebook." He turns to my mother. "Haven't you been helping him with his homework?"

"When?" she asks. "After I've made the dinner,

washed the dishes, given Tyson his bath, done the laundry . . ."

"And what am I doing?" he yells. "Only working from sunup to sundown to support this family."

"Oh, yeah? Well, me, too, buster," she shouts back at him. "Have you forgotten that I work at the hospital all day?"

I take Tyson by the hand and head out of the living room. I figure since they're fighting maybe they'll forget about me.

My father switches his glare from my mother to me and shouts, "Come back here. Where's that notebook?"

I hate when my parents yell at me in front of Tyson. I don't want him to find out what a jerk I am.

Tyson pulls on my hand and begs, "Karate, play karate."

"And no more karate lessons," my father yells. "And no more hanging out with those good-for-nothing friends of yours."

After dinner he tells me, "Brian, there'll be no television for you tonight. You're hitting the books." That's exactly what I want to do with my schoolbooks: Hit them. Tear them. Burn them. Destroy them!

While my parents and Hilary are laughing at Saturday-night sitcoms on TV, I'm in my room copying each of my spelling words twenty-five times.

At ten o'clock my father comes in to check on my work and to test me. "We'll do this every night," he tells me. "I'm checking everything you do." He looks over what I've written so far. " 'Incredible,' " he says. "Just look at that." He points to where I printed "i-n-c-e-r-d-i-b-l-e," and says, "It's 'c-r-e-d,' not 'c-e-r-d.' You misspelled it. Twenty-five times. How are you going to learn if you can't even copy right? And this handwriting. Who can read it?"

"I can," I say.

He yells, "Don't get fresh."

Then he tests me on all the spelling words except "incredible." I get two right and ten wrong.

Later, as I'm falling asleep, I think, "My father's an INCREDIBLY mean man, and I'm an INCREDIBLY stupid boy."

I'm also INCREDIBLY surprised at our meeting with Mr. Bigham on Monday morning. After he shakes hands with my mother and father, he says, "I've asked you here to tell you how bright your son is and to discuss ways we can help him use his intelligence to improve in his schoolwork. Brian is a very smart young man."

"Brian? Smart?" My father looks confused.

"Me?" I say.

"I've always told you he was smart," my mother tells my father.

"I've always told you he was lazy," my father tells my mother.

Are my parents going to start arguing in front of Mr. Bigham?

"I don't think Brian has been lazy," Mr. Bigham says. "I think he's been discouraged." He looks at me. "I'll bet that at the beginning of this school term you promised yourself you would do better in your schoolwork than you did last year. That you would work extra hard. I think you told yourself, 'I can do it.' Then when you tried, all the letters got scrambled, so that you even misspelled your own name on the board." He looks right into my eyes, right into my brain. "Is that what happened?"

"Yes," I whisper. "That's what happened. I said to myself, 'I can do it.' But I couldn't."

I knew then that Mr. Bigham is no ordinary person. In addition to being the strongest man in Sharon or maybe in all of Connecticut, he's a mind reader.

My father says, "I don't understand how you can tell us Brian is smart if he has so much trouble with a simple thing like spelling. I tried helping him with his spelling this weekend. No matter how many times he wrote those words, he couldn't get them right."

Mr. Bigham nods and says, "I know that Brian has a lot of trouble with spelling. But there are different ways of being smart, and some very smart people have trouble with reading the letters of the alphabet and putting numbers in order. Brian is one of them."

That's when Mr. Bigham says he's convinced that I have a learning difference called *dyslexia*, and explains that it's hard for people with dyslexia to learn to read and remember some kinds of things.

"Like the capitals of the states," I say. "And the multiplication tables, even the five timeses."

He smiles. "That's right. That kind of memory work is very challenging for you. For other people, it's as easy as one, two, three."

"People like Isabel Morris," I say.

"Exactly." Mr. Bigham holds up my test papers. "I see from testing Brian that he can understand really difficult ideas. And he thinks in interesting and creative ways." He looks at me as if I'm someone really special. "Did you know," he asks, "that the actors Tom Cruise and Cher are dyslexic? So were Thomas Edison, Albert Einstein, and Leonardo da Vinci. Like them, Brian, you have great intuition. That means you can understand things without going through a lot of steps to get to the idea. You have an excellent mind. There are lots of things you will learn faster and understand better than people whose minds work in a more ordinary way."

Mr. Bigham seems so impressed with my special brain that I don't have the heart to tell him I'd rather have a more ordinary one. One that wouldn't get me in trouble with my parents and that would get me good marks in school. He has all sorts of plans for me and my brain.

First of all he wants my parents to say it's okay for me to take more tests with a specialist to find out more about my learning differences and to make it official on my school records that I'm dyslexic. Next he wants me to start going to the resource room during study period to get help with my homework. "And I'm going to give you extra help, too," he tells me. "We'll find a way to get you over some of these reading problems." He looks me right in the eyeballs. "You're going to have to work hard. Now that I know how interestingly your mind works, I'm going to expect a lot more from you in school. I want you to start making a real contribution to the class. And don't worry, I'll know what kind of questions to ask you."

That's when my father says he will help me at home. Mr. Bigham reads my mind again and says that he thinks my father makes me nervous when he helps me, and asks if my mother could do it.

"I could help him if someone else did the dishes for a change," my mother tells my father.

My father says doing the dishes is a lot easier than helping me with my homework.

Mr. Bigham says that the best help would be if they could hire a tutor to work with me once or twice a week.

My father says that we can't afford it and that, besides, it's up to the school to help me. That's what he pays taxes for.

I'm embarrassed that he says that, but Mr. Bigham agrees with him. Both my parents say it's okay for me to take the special tests.

"Now tell me," Mr. Bigham says, "what are some of the things that you like to do, Brian? What are you good at?"

My mother answers for me. "Brian's good with his hands. He can design and build brilliantly, just like his father and grandfather." She tells him all about the fancy birdhouses I made with Grandpa Al when I was only eight, and how we sold them at the August craft fair on the town green. Mr. Bigham thinks that's a big deal.

"But he should be good at book learning," my father says. "That's what we're here to talk about."

"And what about sports?" Mr. Bigham asks. "Physical activities?"

"Soccer and swimming." My mother's answering for me again.

But Mr. Bigham's looking right at me. "Anything else?" he asks.

"Karate," I answer. "I'm a brown belt."

"A brown belt at your age?" he says. "That's pretty impressive. Listen to me, Brian. No matter how much extra work we load on you, be sure to leave time for building and karate. Promise me that, will you?"

I look at my dad. He shrugs and nods.

I smile at Mr. Bigham and say, "Sure. Why not?"

* * *

Later, at the beginning of recess the Jokers Club beats the seventh graders to the soccer field. For a couple of minutes we have the whole field to ourselves. "You must be in big trouble with Mr. Big," John yells to me as we take positions. "I saw your mother and father in the hall."

Dan throws me the ball. "Maybe you better cool it on the Big Jokes," he says.

I'm about to tell them that I'm not in trouble, but decide they probably aren't very interested in how smart I am. What would I say? "Guess what, I really am Brian the Brain." They'd tease me for sure. None of us do good in school, which is part of why we're such good friends.

"Hey, man," I say as I kick the ball to Richie, "I can handle it." But, I wonder, can I?

That night when I get in bed I lay awake in the dark for a long time, thinking about the meeting with my parents and Mr. Bigham. He said I'm smart, that I'm a good thinker. I remember times in school when I knew the answer before the other kids, but just didn't say it out loud. And I remember the time during fifth-grade science class when we studied how an internal combustion engine works. I knew how it worked as soon as I looked at the thing. I just couldn't have explained it to everyone else the way the teacher did. So no one knew I knew. But, now, because of the test, Mr. Bigham knows I know how to think about a lot of things.

For a while I wonder what my friends would do if they found out I was smart. Would we still be friends? I fall asleep thinking about how neat it would be to get good grades, to be a good reader, and to know the answers in my classes, more answers than even Isabel Morris. And how great it would be to learn anything I wanted to, to become anything I wanted to be: a doctor, or a lawyer, or a scientist who understands everything about the Canada goose.

The next day, during first-period science, Mr. Bigham announces a project that won't be due for months, but that we will start working on right away. "It's an animal-life project," he explains. "Each of you is to pick an animal that you're interested in knowing more about. You will learn all that you can about the animal and report it to the class." Then he asks us what we think would be the best way to learn about an animal. "Any ideas, Brian?" he asks.

He's surprised me. But I think for a moment about the Canada goose and say, "Watch them. See how they communicate with each other."

"Very good," Mr. Bigham says. He writes on the board "Field Study."

Isabel raises her hand. "Reading," she says. Mr. Bigham writes that on the board, while Isabel tells the class about all the research she would do by reading in books and magazines. She even says what part of the library she'll use.

Mr. Bigham says that by the end of the day we should each turn in a piece of paper with the name of the animal we will study on one side, and our own name on the other. I already know my animal.

Next period is journal writing. As we open our journals, Mr. Bigham reminds us, "Write whatever is on your mind. Maybe you want to write down some of the ideas you have about your animal-life project for science. And if you have trouble with spelling or any of the mechanics of writing, don't worry about that during journal writing. Just get your ideas down in any form you can." He looks right at me. "Understood?"

I nod. Then I write on the first page of my journal:

Canada geas are smart. I donet no how there smart, I just no they are. They have a way to live that is smart for them. I like them. I here some honking over the school as I rite this. There going soth for the wintr. They have a go sens of dretion. I have an offul sens of direton and dont no left from right sometimes. When I git older I want to travull, but wat if I git lost all the time?

The next day I spend the whole morning at the high school taking tests with Dr. Ruth Jenner, who knows all about dyslexia. It's a long time to be taking tests, but they're not as hard as I thought they'd be. When I meet up with the other Jokers at lunch, I tell them I missed school because I had a doctor's appointment.

That afternoon Mr. Bigham says, "Resource room people, let's put a move on." Every day, during study period, three of the kids in our class go to the resource room: Jae Kim, a Korean boy who doesn't know English very well; Jenny, who's deaf; and Leonard, who's not so smart since he hit his head in a bike accident. He wasn't wearing a helmet. I always wear my helmet when I ride my bike, but I still have to go to the resource room.

I get up to follow the others out of the room. John looks pretty surprised when I pass his desk. I hunch over, walk with my feet pointed out like a duck, and pull a dumb-looking face. He thinks what I want him to think — that I'm making fun of going to the resource room. He laughs. Dan and Richie laugh, too, and so do a few other kids. The Jokers Club members scratch their heads.

Mr. Bigham doesn't laugh or say anything. He just looks at me and raises his right eyebrow. I stand up straight and leave the room as fast as I can without running.

The resource room is smaller than a regular classroom, which is okay because there are only a few kids in there at a time. Ms. Crandal starts out by talking to each kid. When she gets to me, she asks what my biggest problem is with homework.

"Social studies," I tell her.

She asks to see the notes I took in class that day. Right away there's a big problem — neither of us can read what I wrote.

"I can't listen and write at the same time," I tell her.

"A lot of people have that problem," she says. "See me at the end of the session. I have something that will help you."

When the bell rings and Jenny, Jae, and Leonard have left, Ms. Crandal reaches into her desk drawer. "This should help you with note taking," she says. She pulls out a tape recorder and hands it to me.

I stare at it. "How's a tape recorder going to help?"

She explains that from now on I'll sit in the first row in social studies class and record the part of class when everyone else is taking notes. That way she and I can listen to the lecture later, and she'll help me write out my notes.

At the bike rack after school, Dan marks down my two points plus one Big Point in the Operation J.D.B.R. score book.

"You're way ahead," John tells me. "How do you do it?"

"It's easy," I say. "I'm just myself." I screw my body and face back into my idiot look and they all laugh again.

Richie pats me on the back. "Poor Toomey, you got to go to the retard room."

John says, "Hey, dudes, let's go over to the hideout now. There's still some of those pretzels. We'll pick up sodas on the way."

"I can't, man," Dan tells him. "I've got to go right home. My father said."

"Count me out," I say as I get on my bike. "I gotta do something for my mother."

No way am I going to tell them that I couldn't go to the hideout after school because I have to go home and study. Or that I have to use a tape recorder in Mr. Dithers' social studies class because I can't even copy notes off the board right.

5

John: 2 Points
+ 1 Big Point
+ 2 Isabel Points

Thursday afternoon Mr. Bigham holds up our slips of papers for the animal-life project. "For this project," he says, "you will be working with partners." He explains that whenever two people put down the same animal, they'll work together. And when only one person chose a particular animal, they'll work with someone who has a similar animal. Like someone doing dolphins will work with someone doing whales. He hasn't looked at the other side of our papers to see who the people are, but has divided the papers up just by the kind of animal.

Dan and Richie get put together because they both put down raccoon. Probably because of the raccoon that got into our food supply at the hideout.

After announcing the horse people, the turtle people, the tiger and leopard people, and the cow people, Mr. Bigham says, "Let's see, we have two

Canada goose here." He turns my paper over, "One is Brian Toomey. And the other is — "

Before he turns the next paper over, Isabel shouts, "Oh, no. Not fair."

" — Isabel Morris."

"Not *her*," I say as I slump in my seat. "No way."

Everyone in the room is howling, but the Jokers Club aren't scratching their heads. Mr. Bigham doesn't get points for making jokes.

Besides, it isn't a joke. Isabel really is my partner. Ten minutes later, the class breaks up into twos to work on their animal projects. Isabel Morris and I push our desks together and sit face to face. While the rest of the pairs are having fun, we're glaring and being angry at one another and at Mr. Bigham for his big stupid idea. No one else in the room hates being partners as much as Isabel and me.

Mr. Bigham is smiling and being friendly as he goes from group to group, asking the kids questions and helping them do what he calls "Phase One: Organizing for Research." Isabel and I just sit there not saying a word to one another. When Mr. Bigham gets to us, I look up at him, but I don't smile.

"What's the problem here?" Mr. Bigham asks.

Isabel looks at her big hands and mumbles, "I can't work with him. He won't do anything. I'll have to do it all. And then when it's time for the report in class, he'll mess it up and I won't get an A."

"Oh?" Mr. Bigham says as he squats on his haunches so he can look her in the face. "You know, Isabel," he says, "this project isn't graded only on the final report. It's also graded on how well people work together."

Isabel groans.

He continues. "And it's graded on how many different ways you use to gather information, and on how creative you are in teaching the rest of the class about the Canada goose. Besides, I hope you do this project because it's interesting to you. You're not just working for a grade."

"But he won't do any work," Isabel tells him.

"We can't work together," I say.

"Why are you interested in the Canada goose, Brian?" Mr. Bigham asks me.

I tell him — not Isabel — about how much I like to watch and listen to them when they migrate. That I think they are neat.

"What would you like to know about them?" he asks.

"Everything. Like where they have nests, and how far they fly when they migrate, and who their enemies are."

"There're three good questions," he said. "Maybe you should write those questions down, Isabel."

"I already know the answers," she tells me in that snotty Isabel-voice.

"You do?" I ask. "So where do they have their nests?"

"Around marshy places," she says. "Marshy means wet."

"I know what marshy means," I tell her. "But where are the marshy places?"

"I don't know *exactly* where."

"Well," I tell her, "I want to know *exactly* where. And especially if there are any in Sharon."

Mr. Bigham unfolds his six feet four inches and stands up. He asks me, "Do you have any more questions?"

"I do," Isabel says. "How long is this project going to last, and how many times do I have to work with him?"

Mr. Bigham looks annoyed. "I meant questions about the Canada goose," he tells us. "Make a list of those questions."

He claps his hands once to get everyone's attention. "Class," he says, "this is a two-month-long project. You will meet with your partners in class for fifteen minutes every two weeks, but I expect you to work together outside of school, too."

Isabel moans. I groan.

Mr. Bigham continues. "If your animals are local, include some field study, do firsthand observation."

"How can I observe my animal?" Charlene asks. "It's an ape."

"Just watch Isabel," John yells out.

Some kids laugh, and Richie and Dan roar as they scratch their heads. I scratch my head, too, but I don't laugh because I'm facing Isabel.

"Stop it," she hisses at me.

"What?" I ask. "I'm not laughing."

She has tears in her eyes, but she glares at me with a fury that could kill.

I stop scratching because I know by her look that she thinks Dan and Richie and I are mimicking an ape — Isabel the Ape — by scratching our heads.

Mr. Bigham stops being friendly and happy about his idea of putting us in groups. "Enough," he says in his low, firm voice. The class quiets down. He takes three big, slow steps over to where John sits. John keeps grinning, but he has to be scared to death. All Mr. Bigham does is give him the first detention of the year.

At the end of the day, as the rest of us are filing out of the room, Mr. Bigham stops me. "Look, Brian, I know you and Isabel aren't exactly best friends."

"I'll say."

"It's just a coincidence that you two ended up together."

"I know."

"I hope she'll learn something from you."

I look up into Mr. Bigham's eyes for signs of craziness. But his dark brown eyes are clear and calm. I ask him, "How's she going to learn anything from me? She thinks I'm the stupidest thing to ever walk the face of the earth."

He smiles. "But you're not. You're very smart."

"She hates me. I hate her."

"Well," he says with a little laugh, "you have something in common."

"Hate?"

"No." He winks at me. "The Canada goose."

I think, I don't like Canada geese anymore. Not if Isabel Morris has anything to do with them.

Mr. Bigham pats me on the shoulder, "Don't forget about your tutoring session with Mrs. Samuels in room 104."

I walk down the hall thinking about how complicated my life has become since I found out I was smart and "learning different."

"Hey, man, put a move on." It's Dan. He and Richie are standing at the end of the corridor, waiting for me. Just then, John comes charging down the hall. He grabs me by the arm and we run — right past the room where I'm supposed to meet my tutor. As the four of us push through the front doors, we're cheering because John got out of detention faster than ever.

At the bike rack John tells us, "Five Joker points for me. And I have a new name for Isabel. Ape."

"You mean 'Is-a-ape,' instead of 'Is-a-bel'?" I ask.

"Yeah," John says. "Exactly. Is-a-ape. Is-a-ape."

We all laugh. He slaps me on the back. "Poor

Toomey. What rotten luck having Is-a-ape for a partner."

"How'd you get out of detention so fast?" Dan asks John.

"I told him to go stuff it."

Richie's amazed that John dared say that to Mr. Bigham. But I don't believe it, not for a second. I bet Dan doesn't believe it, either. I think John told some whopping lie to get out of detention — like his mother is in the hospital or something.

John and I ride home on our bikes, like always. After he turns the corner onto his street, I turn around and ride back to school.

When I get to the tutor's room I'm all sweaty, out of breath, and half an hour late.

"Well, there you are," Mrs. Samuels says when I come running in. "You must be Brian. I was afraid you weren't coming."

She stands up and walks right up to me. "You surprised to see what an old lady I am?" she asks.

I nod because Mrs. Samuels looks like she's about a hundred years old.

"I'm retired from regular teaching," she explains. "I've volunteered to tutor you. I want to help you, but to do that, you must be here. You're very late."

I say I'm sorry, and she promises she won't tell my parents if I promise it won't happen again. She gives me a piece of homemade banana bread and a bottle of apple juice so I'll have energy for working with her.

Then she hands me a pad and pencil and says, "Let's start at the beginning. I'd like you to write the alphabet for me, Brian."

Next she has me read letters off flash cards and tell her their sounds. It's when she's explaining the difference between consonants and vowels that I mumble, "This is baby work." I'm afraid I might have hurt her feelings, but she doesn't seem to mind at all.

"This work is elementary, I admit," she says. "But it's going to lead you right into more advanced work." She pats me on the back. "I wish you could see into the future, young man, because then you would see that after we've worked together for a couple of years, you are going to be able to put any ideas you have into words — written words."

Years! I think. It's going to take *years*? I feel awful. I want to ask Mrs. Samuels why, if I'm so smart, it will take years for me to learn to read and write as good as even Richie or John.

Mrs. Samuels is happy about teaching me to read. She isn't worried about how long it will take. "I can help you," she says. "You show great promise."

At the end of my lesson, while I'm watching her set up a notebook for my "phonics" homework, I wonder what will happen if my friends find out about my afternoon sessions with a tutor. I wonder what they would think if they knew I'm taking school seriously. That I'm not a true Joker after all.

6

Richie: 2 Points + 2 Isabel Points

"**H**ow's it going 'Brain'?" my sister Hilary asks as she passes me a baked potato. I kick her under the table. "Hey, quit it," she yells.

"Brian," my father snaps.

"She's bugging me," I tell him.

"Just be quiet and eat your dinner," he says.

Hilary can keep talking, though. "Mom," she says, "I have to go to the library right after dinner."

"Hilary," my mother tells her, "you have to help with the dishes before you go anywhere. Now that I'm helping Brian with his homework, you'll have to pitch in more than ever."

"If you're helping Brian, then Brian should do the dishes," she says.

"While you help your father with the dishes and I do the laundry, Brian will be busy giving Tyson his bath and putting him to bed."

Old Hilary doesn't give up. "Mom, I have to go to the library to do research for history class.

Schoolwork is my job. You always said."

"Doing the dishes is your job, too," my father tells her.

"No one ever helps me with *my* homework," Hilary says.

"No one has to," my father answers with his first smile of the evening.

"It's not Brian's fault," my mother says. "After all, he didn't ask to be dyslexic."

I mumble, "I didn't ask to be born, either."

My father glares at me.

"Everyone's trying to help you, Brian," my mother says. "Don't start trouble."

I don't enjoy my dinner very much after that, but giving Tyson a bath isn't half bad. When he's all sweet-smelling and dressed in his baseball pajamas, I lift him up to pop him into the crib. When he sees where he's headed, he starts kicking and cries, "Brian rock Tyson. Mommy rocks Tyson."

I sit down in the rocking chair with him. He clutches his ratty old blanket and looks up at me. "Brian read," he orders. "Mommy reads."

I pick out a "Frog and Toad" book from the pile next to the rocker and open it. I show him a picture of Frog and Toad walking together. "Look," I say, "they're walking down the road."

"Read words," he orders.

So I read by sounding out the words and following the syllable rules that my tutor taught me. Whenever Toad is talking in the story, I make my voice low. When it's Frog's turn, I start and end his speech with "Rib-it."

Tyson loves this and doesn't even notice that I'm a slow reader.

The next night I read him "Frog and Toad" again. By the third night I'm pretty sick of reading the same book over and over and decide to go to the library and pick out some new books for him. Ones I'm sure I can read.

Friday Mr. Dithers announces that we're starting a unit on the American Revolution and we should take notes. "Brian," he says, "I understand that you are to sit in the front row. Please change places with Irene."

As I pass Dan on the way to the front, he asks, "What'd you do?"

I shrug my shoulders and whisper back, "I guess because I'm always fooling around."

I sit down. As soon as people have stopped staring at me, I take out the tape recorder Ms. Crandal gave me. At home I wrapped it in a paper napkin and practiced pressing the record button without looking at it. With this disguise I figure no one will notice what I'm doing.

As I'm putting the napkin-wrapped recorder on my desk, Mr. Dithers says to the class, "Whenever the class takes notes, Brian will record my lecture.

As you probably know, he has a learning disability. He also will be able to spend as long as he needs to on tests."

I slump down in my seat. How could he do this to me?

"No fair," Jason calls out. "Why should he have more time?"

Mr. Dithers spends five minutes lecturing us on how everyone has different abilities and learning styles, and makes me feel like a world-class jerk.

"I don't have any choice," I tell the other Jokers at lunch. "If I don't go to the tutor and get better grades, my dad'll kill me. I can't do anything about it until I live on my own."

"Hey, man, just say no," John says. "Your folks won't kick you out."

"You don't know my father," I tell him.

"Yes I do," John answers. "He's no different from any other father. You're just wimping out, man. You got to start talking back more. Look at him like you'd beat him up if he dared lay a hand on you. Use your karate on him. A tutor? Give me a break."

Before I can think of a way of changing the subject, Isabel comes clumping past our table with her lunch tray. Richie calls out, "Hey, Isabel, you dropped something." She automatically leans over her tray and looks at the floor. At that instant, Richie does a handfart.

A whole table of eighth-grade guys hear it and laugh. We start scratching our heads. Isabel glares at me as if it's all my fault.

"Two points," Richie boasts, "plus two Is-a-ape points. Did you see her? She thought she really did it."

"No she didn't," I say. "She was mad."

"Maybe we should get extra points if we get someone really mad," Richie says.

I think that's a dumb idea, but don't say so.

"Hey, it's Friday," Dan reminds us. "We can all go to the hideout. Do you have tutoring?" he asks me.

"I'm not a prisoner," I tell them. "I can still go to the hideout on Fridays."

"But I can't today," John says.

"Do you have to stay after?" Dan asks.

"Me? Nah. Bigham won't pull that on me again. I just got some business to take care of. You got trouble with that?"

Dan shakes his head.

"I can't go, either," Richie says. "I got to, you know, go someplace. The dentist."

"Better give me the week's moolah now," John says. We each give him two dollars, which he rolls in a wad and sticks in his back pocket. "I'll put it in the tin when we get to the hideout tomorrow," he tells us.

After school I hang out with Dan for a little while,

but he wants to go watch TV and I want to stay outdoors. I'm riding my bike around the shopping center thinking maybe I'll just go home and take Tyson to the playground when I hear, "HONK HONK." I look up. The Canada geese are on the move. I start going in the direction of the big goose V in the sky. Then I get this great idea about my report on the geese.

I cycle as fast as I can on Route 343 toward the highest building around. The Colgate mansion. I slow down when I remember the rule about not going to the hideout unless everyone can go. But, I remind myself, the hideout is in the gardener's shed, not the big house. I just won't go near the shed. I pedal full out the rest of the way.

After I hide my bike behind the garage, I sneak into the mansion through the cellar window John pried open last summer. The cellar smells like old socks and is darker than I thought it would be. I get upstairs fast. I don't count rooms this time, or look around. I'm too scared. On the top floor I climb the ladder, push the hatch open, and pull myself onto the roof.

Before I even look around I take my tape recorder out of my knapsack and turn the tape over to side B. Mr. Dithers is on side A, and the Canada geese sounds will be on side B. Now that I'm on the roof, I'm not afraid. I like being up here where I can see my town laid out like a map.

I'm looking for the roof of my house when I hear "HONK. HONK" behind me. I push the record button on the tape recorder and hold it up to the sky, microphone toward the V of geese heading my way. Then I get an idea and turn the microphone back toward me and say clearly, "The sounds of the Canada goose, four P.M., October 2, 1992, as heard by Brian Albert Toomey. The geese are flying in a southerly direction."

They fly directly toward me, honking like crazy. As they get close to the mansion, they take a dive. Are they going to land on the roof? I lie down on my belly so I won't scare them off. When I lift my head just enough to take a peek, I see that they haven't landed around me after all. I still hear honking, so I crawl over to the edge of the roof and look down. At least a hundred Canada geese have landed in the field next to the gardener's shed.

I describe into the recorder what the geese look like and how they're feeding. I stop talking and try to count them, but it's hard to keep track because they keep moving around to feed.

BANG! The crack of a gunshot explodes through the window of the shed. It sends the geese up and out of there with a *swoosh* of wings and a thousand honks. I scan the field. No dead bodies. The shot missed its mark, and all the geese have escaped.

Five guys come out of the shed. Before I have a chance to think that some other kids have found our hideout, I see that two of the boys are Richie and John. The other three are eighth graders. Real troublemakers — Teddy, Steve, and Mac. Mac is holding a hunting rifle. He shouts curses at the fleeing geese and laughs. John and Richie have brought other people to our hideout!

I lie as flat as I can, slide away from the edge of the roof, and lay there listening to them laughing and talking. With the honking geese gone I can overhear what they say.

"There're more than twenty rooms in there and no one's using them," John says.

"Now *that* should be the clubhouse," one of the eighth graders says. Is it Steve?

"Come on. We'll give you a tour," Richie says.

"You got a way to get in, John?" Mac asks.

"What do you think?" John answers.

My heart jumps. I hear their evil laughter as they run toward the mansion. BANG! Another gunshot.

As I look around the roof trying to decide what to do, I notice the open hatch to the top floor. I crawl over to it, and close it. I sit on it and think about all the mean things Teddy, Steve, and Mac have done to animals and to kids. What would they do if they found me?

An hour passes. Minute by minute it's getting darker and colder. I look at my watch. 6:03 P.M. I'm already late for dinner. It starts to rain.

I get this awful thought: What if they decide to

stay all night? None of those guys is afraid of his parents. I tell myself, "Brian, you've got to find a way out of this. Even if five nutso guys are roaming around inside with a gun." I picture in my mind the layout of the mansion with its twenty-seven rooms and network of hallways. I see it like an architectural design my dad would make. Then I imagine myself in this plan and try to figure a route for getting back down the four flights of stairs and through the cellar window without being seen.

I shiver from the cold, and sneeze. "You jerk," I say out loud. "You're not inside. You're outside." In my mind's eye I move the imaginary me to where I really am — on the roof. *Outside* the house. I add what's on the outside of the house to my plan. Three porches. And a fire escape that goes from the roof to the beginning of the second story where I know there should be a ladder that can be dropped to the ground. I picture the pattern of the fire escape and compare it to the layout of the rooms. It follows the line of hall windows.

I get off the hatch, walk to the edge of the roof, and climb onto the fire escape. Careful not to slip on the wet metal, I start my descent — stair by stair. At each landing I crawl under the window to keep out of sight from the guys inside.

At the second floor I lean over to unhinge the ladder that flips out to the ground. It's rusted in place and won't budge. The drop to the ground is about twenty feet. I hear laughter and loud voices. I turn and see the beam of a flashlight approaching the window. If I jump, I risk breaking a leg. I estimate it's a three-foot leap to the roof of the porch. I picture the porch with its smooth, rounded columns. I leap the three feet and hit the porch with a loud thump.

"What's that?" a voice from inside shouts. I hear the sound of a window opening.

I run to the edge of the roof, hoist myself over, and slide down the column to the porch. I run across the lawn as fast as a goose flies. Will they think that I'm an animal and shoot? I round the corner of the garage, jump on my bike, and ride through the woods and onto the highway. I never look back, and even though it hurts to breathe, I don't slow down until I'm riding down my own street.

As I'm putting my bike into the garage, I wonder if tomorrow John will tell us about the guys he brought to the hideout.

But the next day I can't meet the Jokers at the clubhouse. I can't go to my karate lessons, either. I have to stay home the whole day because I was an hour late for dinner. I also have a terrible cold.

Sunday morning I go over to Dan's. This is one of my favorite things to do. Dan's father is not as nervous and grumpy as my dad. And he makes the best Sunday brunch, with homemade blueberry pancakes. I'd like to bring Tyson with me sometime so he can see what a family is like where the mother and father aren't always arguing with one another and yelling at the kids.

After breakfast Dan and I go to his room to build a model airplane.

Dan says that he and Richie and John waited for me at the clubhouse on Saturday. That it was real boring and after a little while of just sitting around feeling cold and being quiet, John had said maybe it was time to close the hideout for the year. "He said especially since you can hardly ever come."

"So he's blaming me," I say. "He's the one who has new friends."

"What new friends?" Dan asks.

I tell him that John and Richie went to the hideout without us and that they took eighth graders. He doesn't believe me until I play him the tape recording.

"I'm afraid of those guys," Dan says.

"I don't even like them," I tell him. "And they're in trouble all the time. Big trouble."

Dan's looking sad. "But John and Richie and you and me. We're best friends."

I feel pretty bummed out myself. I'm thinking that I don't trust John with our money anymore. But just thinking that makes me feel sad and sort of sick to my stomach, so I don't say it out loud. Instead,

I tell Dan, "I don't like Operation J.D.B.R. that much anymore. It brings me more grief than relief."

"It's hard for you to fool around in school now, anyway," Dan says. "I don't blame you for being afraid of your father. I hope you get better grades."

"Me, too. It'd make life a lot easier."

"I can do better work in school, too," Dan says. "I was afraid you wouldn't be my friend if I did."

"I don't care if you study," I tell him.

"I know," he says. "But John and Richie'd be real pissed if I started to be good in school."

"Are you afraid of them, too?" I ask.

He nods. "Yeah, a little."

"But people shouldn't be afraid of their friends."

"If you're afraid of someone, maybe they're not such a good friend," Dan adds.

"Maybe not," I agree.

7

John: 2 Points
+ 1 Big Point
+ 2 Is-a-ape Points

Thursday Mr. Bigham tells us to work with our animal-life project partners. When Isabel and I are sitting face to face, she shoves a pile of handwritten pages across her desk onto mine. "Here's what I did," she says. "I spent all day Saturday at the library. I did research from four books and six magazine articles. You can read my notes."

I glance down and pretend to be reading line after line of Isabel's neat script. She leans foward and hisses, "I suppose you didn't do anything."

"I did so," I hiss back. "I did plenty."

"Like what? Read a baby article in some children's magazine?"

"I did field study," I tell her. "On a roof. I watched the geese eating. I made a tape recording."

"I don't believe you. No way did you do that."

I reach into my knapsack and put my cassette recorder between us and say, "Oh, yeah? Here's the evidence."

She snorts. "I still don't believe you."

Now I'm seriously angry. I push the play button. "HONK, HONK. HONK, HONK," blasts from the machine.

Before I can get the volume turned to a normal level, "HONK, HONK. HONK, HONK" is drowning out all the other sounds in the classroom, and everyone is staring at us. By the time Mr. Bigham reaches our desk, I've turned the recorder off.

"Sorry," I tell him. "It's my field study tape."

Mr. Bigham isn't angry. He's smiling as he takes the recorder from me and holds it up to show the class. "Listen up," he tells them. "Brian recorded his field observations. Let's hear what he taped."

Isabel holds out her pile of papers. "Mr. Bigham," she says, "I took these notes at the library. On Saturday."

But Mr. Bigham's already turned on the tape recorder and my taped voice is booming through the room: *The sounds of the Canada goose, four P.M., October 2, 1992, as heard by Brian Albert Toomey. The geese are flying in a southerly direction.*

"This is terrific," Mr. Bigham says above the sound of honking geese. Then he stops the recorder to say, "Did you hear, class, how Brian made a verbal note of the date and the time? Good work, Brian."

I put out my hand to take back the tape recorder, but Mr. Bigham's not about to give it up.

He looks down at me. "You should have given the place, too, Brian. Where did you go to make this recording?"

"On a roof," Isabel answers.

"But where is the roof?" Mr. Bigham asks. "That's an important piece of information."

"Just somewhere," I say. "I'll put it in my final report."

"Good enough," he says. He looks around at the other students. "Class," he says, "this tape is a terrific example of the kind of research I'd like you to do. Let's listen to the rest of it."

I slip down in my seat. Everyone is paying attention. Even John. Especially John.

Mr. Bigham turns the tape recorder back on and my voice continues: *"The geese just flew over me. They are bigger and more powerful than I ever thought. Their white chests look gold in the afternoon light. They're landing in the field. I see that they are eating leftovers from the corn that grew in the field this summer. But not all the geese are eating. A few birds aren't eating. They are watching, looking in every direction. Are they guards? One bird that seems to be guarding the others is eating now, and another goose near him is keeping an eye out for trouble. Are they taking turns? Will the guard goose see me? Will I scare these strong birds away from their dinner?"* Dan and I make eye contact and I know that we're thinking the same thing, that in a second the gunshot recorded on the tape will go off. Then what questions will Mr. Bigham ask? And what will John do when he figures out that I was on the roof of the Colgate mansion, that I saw him with the eighth-grade boys, and that I recorded them using a gun?

CRASH. Dan tips over his desk. The bang of it hitting the floor drowns out the sound of the gunshot on the recording. I think how lucky I am to have a good friend like Dan.

"Sorry, Mr. Bigham," Dan says as he sets his desk upright again. On the tape the geese are honking like crazy as they flap away from the gunshot.

"That's all I did about geese," I shout to Mr. Bigham. He switches off the tape recorder just before the part where John, Richie, and the eighth graders come shouting out of the gardener's shed. Mr. Bigham praises me again and finally hands the recorder back to me.

"That was pretty good," Isabel tells me. "Those birds that guard while the others eat are called sentinels."

Before the rest of the class gets back to work on their own projects, John raises his hand. "Mr. Bigham, sir," he says, "may I ask a question about the project?" Since the only question John has asked in school since first grade is "May I be excused?" everyone is listening to hear what he's going to say.

Mr. Bigham is surprised, too. "Of course, John, what is it?"

"If you have an idea of a different animal you'd like to study, can you change?"

"Well, yes, if you have a good reason for changing. What animal would you like to study and why?"

John is looking right at me when he says, "I'd like to study teachers' pets, sir, because it's an endangered species."

Enough kids laugh for Richie to start scratching his head. So does Danny. John is still looking at me. I know I'm supposed to scratch my head if he's made a good joke. But I don't scratch, for two reasons. One is because out of the corner of my eye I can see an angry look on Isabel's face that tells me she thinks that Richie and Dan are scratching to make fun of her, Isabel-the-Ape. The other reason is that I'm the one John thinks is a teacher's pet, which is against rule number two of Operation J.D.B.R. I especially don't feel like laughing because John said I belong to an endangered species. Does that mean I've gone from being his friend to being on his hit list?

Mr. Bigham says, "Enough."

The class quiets down. Everyone but Isabel. She jumps to her feet, glares over at Richie and Dan, and yells, "I hate you. I hate you." She stamps her feet. "You're . . . you're . . . stupid jackasses. That's the animal you are. A jackass." A few kids are laughing. The rest of us are too shocked. Perfect-student Isabel is screaming, stamping her feet, and calling someone a jackass. In Mr. Bigham's room! It's hard to believe.

Mr. Bigham reaches her before she has time to stamp her feet again. He puts an arm around her shoulder. I hear him say, "Come on, Isabel. We're going into the hall." As he walks her toward the door, he tells the class, "Group work is over for today. Put your seats back in their regular places, take out your math workbooks, and do the problems on page twenty-nine. AND NOT ONE SOUND FROM YOU." It's the first time Mr. Bigham has raised his voice to us.

As soon as he's out of the room with Isabel, John says, "The ape's gone mad."

The only one who laughs is Richie. John shakes his head, mumbles "bunch of wimps," leans his chair back on two legs, and drums on his desk with two pencils. The rest of us do the math problems.

"So, man," John says to me when we meet at the bike rack after school. "How come you didn't scratch? I scored good."

"I thought we weren't going to make jokes on each other," I say.

"Well, looks like we are," John says. "Write down my score, Dan." Dan takes the little notebook out of his back pocket and writes what John dictates. "Two points, plus one Big Joke point, plus two Is-a-ape points."

"How come you get Is-a-ape points?" Dan asks. "You were calling Brian a teacher's pet, not her."

"Come on," John says. "Didn't you see her? She went crazy."

Richie adds, "She was foaming at the mouth, man."

I say, "That's because whenever we signal each other, she thinks we're making fun of her by scratching like an ape."

John laughs like that's the funniest thing he's ever heard. Richie and Dan think it's pretty funny, too. I'm sorry I told them.

"That's beautiful," John says. "Every time we scratch, she thinks we're making fun of her."

"Maybe we should change our signal," I say.

"Why?" he challenges me.

"So we won't get into so much trouble with Mr. Bigham," I answer.

"Bigham really scares you, doesn't he?" John says. "Afraid you won't be teacher's pet anymore?"

I hate that he calls me that again. I don't see anything funny in making fun of people, especially your friends or even people like Isabel. But I don't tell the guys that. I go back into the building for my tutoring session with Mrs. Samuels. Dan's the only one who says good-bye to me. Richie and John are already riding off on their bikes, probably to meet their eighth-grade pals. I turn around when I reach the door and see Dan racing on his bike to catch up with them.

It's hard to concentrate on the rules for spelling and breaking words into syllables when all your best friends are turning on you. I feel rotten. It's been a lot of years that I've been hanging out and playing with John and Richie. We have this plan to buy a van together when we turn eighteen and drive all over the country, camping out and having a great time. Dan's only been friends with us for a year, but he's going to come on the trip, too. I figure the way things are now, the three of them will go without me. My tutoring hour seems about ten hours long. When it's finally over and I leave school, I see Dan back at the bike rack, waiting for me.

"I thought you went with John and Richie," I say.

"I couldn't catch up. I yelled to them, but they didn't hear me." He looks sad. "Or maybe they did hear me and pretended they didn't."

"Probably," I agree.

"Do you think they went back to our hideout with those other guys?" he asks.

"Probably."

Dan says, "I'm sorry I scratched my head when

John made a joke about you. I wanted to catch up with them to tell them that. To say we shouldn't make jokes about one another."

"Thanks," I say. I jump on my bike. "Come on. I'll race you."

"To my house," Dan adds. "Maybe you can stay for dinner."

When I call my mother from Dan's, she says I have to come right home and shouldn't I be doing my homework instead of playing.

"But I just went to my tutor," I protest. "Don't I ever get time to hang out?" I tell her how great I did in school with my project, and that she can ask Dan.

But she doesn't want to talk to Dan. "Be home in ten minutes," is all she says.

For dinner we have spaghetti with sauce from a jar, cold chicken, and string beans left over from last night.

We don't talk too much when we eat because you never know when you'll say something that'll make my father angry. My mother says he's grumpy at dinner because he works so hard to support us and because he has a bad back. We're almost finished eating when she tells my dad, "We got a postcard from your father today."

"Why'd you wait so long to tell me?" my father

asks. That's what I mean about being grumpy.

"Lemme see it," Hilary says.

My mother hands me the postcard to hand to Hilary. It's a picture of an alligator wearing sunglasses. I turn the card over.

Hilary grabs it from me. "I asked first," she says. "I'll read it out loud."

"How's he doing?" my father asks my mother. "Has he hooked up with a rich Florida widow yet?"

"Listen to the card," my mother answers.

I love my grandpa Albert. I like him better than my father, his own son. After my grandma died last year, Grandpa Al didn't tell so many jokes or do the neat things I like to do with him, like fishing. Now he's in Florida visiting his brother and "checking it out."

"Brian," he told me before he left, "a change of scene is what I need. I'll see the sea and then we'll see." He put his arm around me and gave me a hug. "Your grandma wouldn't want me to be feeling so sad. I just can't help it." His eyes filled with up with tears.

I miss Grandma, too, but I don't think about her all the time the way he does. I don't believe he's looking for any kind of a widow to hook up with, even a rich Florida one.

"So read it," I tell Hilary.

She reads, " 'Dear Family.' " She stops to laugh.

72

"Look," she says, showing my father the card. "He spelled dear like the animal, d-e-e-r."

"You know what he means," my father says. "Just read it."

" 'Dear family,' " Hilary begins again. " 'Here I am in sunny Florida.' " She looks up again. "He spelled sunny with only one 'n.' And here's a word I can't even read. Doesn't he know how to spell?"

"Would you shut up and read the card," my father scolds.

"How can I shut up and read?" Hilary asks.

My father reaches over and grabs the card from Hilary. He reads it to himself, then looks up at us. "He's fine," he says. "No rich widows yet."

"Can I have it back, Dad?" Hilary asks.

"Not if you're going to make fun of your grandfather."

"I'm sorry," Hilary says. "I wasn't making fun. It's just that he spells like Brian. I didn't know that."

My mother tells my father, "You're not such a great speller yourself, Roy Toomey. In fact, you spell just like your father." She smiles at me. "And they both make the same kinds of mistakes you make, Brian. I remember the first Valentine's Day card your father sent me, above the printed verse he wrote, 'Deer Ellen.' D-e-e-r. The same mistake!"

"Would you all just knock it off about people's mistakes," my father growls. He pushes his chair away from the table and gets up. "I've got some calls to make. Hilary, you'll do the dishes alone tonight."

"No fair," Hilary protests to my mother as soon as my father's out of earshot. "He's mad at me because everyone in this family but you and me are lousy spellers? It's not fair."

My mother sighs. "Hilary," she says, "drop it. Brian, give Tyson his bath."

I peel spaghetti off Tyson's face and bib and pull him out of his high chair. "Want to take a bath, Tyson?" I ask.

"Swim, swim," Tyson says. I hold him out so he can pretend he's swimming through the air. As I pass my father's place, I grab the postcard.

That night, before I start my homework, I stare at the postcard. The handwriting looks just like mine. I read.

Deer Famly,

Chears from suny Floraid. Whether is great. Floraid is an incerible place. Josie would have loved it. Hows my wonderful grand children?
Be home soon. Uncle Joe sends love to.

Grandpa Al

I wonder, is Grandpa dyslexic? Does he have the same learning difference I have? Maybe my Dad is dyslexic, too. Maybe I inherited it the way I inherited my mom's blue eyes and my dad's long legs. Has Tyson inherited dyslexia, too? I decide that if he has, I'll be sure he doesn't have to wait until sixth grade to get special help like I did.

8

Brian: 2 Points

It's the morning of the first big test in social studies. While I'm riding my bike down our street, I review the causes for the Revolutionary War. I only remember two. I decide to go to the resource room after lunch and review everything with Ms. Crandal one more time. I hate tests. When I take a test, my head pounds. I get so nervous about not understanding the questions that the letters on the page look like a foreign language. I can't read the simplest word.

As I turn the corner onto Main Street, I swerve into the curb to keep from crashing into three bikers going in the opposite direction. It's John, Richie, and Dan.

"Hey, man, where are you going?" Richie asks.

"Where does it look like I'm going?" I ask back. "Where're you going?"

"To get you, man," John says. "Didn't you hear the radio? No school today."

The only reason they ever cancel school over the radio is for snow days. I look up at the bright blue October sky and ask, "How come?"

Richie says, "There's some kind of an emergency with the furnace. They've got to fix it, but it's too dangerous to do with kids in the building. So no school."

I look around at my friends' happy faces and ask, "This is true? You're not kidding?"

"Scout's honor," John answers.

"Yahoo!" I shout. "No social studies test."

I turn my bike around and we "yahoo" and shout cheers all the way to Route 343. By 8:30, when we'd usually be starting math class, we're hanging out in our hideout drinking sodas and passing around potato chips. Through the shed window I count five blue jays in the apple orchard. It feels like summer again. I think, these three guys are my pals. John and I had a little misunderstanding, but now we'll get it back together. I decide to forgive John for bringing the eighth graders to our hideout and for embarrassing me in front of the whole class. I take a handful of chips and pass the bag to Richie.

"Man," Richie says. "This is more like it. That school was beginning to bug me."

"Bigham is bugging me," John says. "He's getting on my nerves. I'm going to have to do something to put him in his place."

"I don't think you should mess with him," Dan says. "He's too awesome."

"Are you guys still afraid of him?" John asks. "Didn't I tell you he's not going to do anything to us? He wouldn't dare. It's his first year here, he's got to do good or he's out the door, like Ms. Olgey."

"I don't know," Dan comments.

"You guys are such wimps," John continues. "Just because he's black, you think he's dangerous. You're being prejudiced. Especially you, Dan."

I want to say that the reason we don't have to be afraid of Mr. Bigham is because he's a nice guy, but I keep my mouth shut. I don't want to be called a teacher's pet again.

"Listen, you guys," John says, "if I do pull a joke on Bigham, I expect all of you to be behind me."

"What are you going to do?" I ask.

He crumbles up the empty potato chip bag, tosses it to me, and says, "I'll think of something." His grin says he already has. I don't like the idea of playing a joke on Mr. Bigham, especially now that he's going through so much trouble to help me.

"So what're we going to do now?" Richie asks.

"Let's hang out in the big house," John suggests.

I think, but don't say, just like you and Richie did with Mac and those other eighth-grade clowns?

A few minutes later we're sliding around in our sock feet on the front hall marble floor.

"Hey, John," Richie says, "this hallway is bigger than your whole house."

John puts his finger to his lip. "*Sh-hh*. Don't use names. The place might be bugged with tape recorders." Did he look at me in a funny way when he said that?

"Let's play hide-and-seek," Richie says.

"Forget it," I say. "That's a baby game."

But John says, "It won't be a baby game in this house, with all these rooms. It'll be freak-out time. Let's do it. Dan, you be first. Close your eyes and count to fifty, and we'll all hide."

Dan closes his eyes and starts counting. "One-two-three . . ."

I don't trust John and Richie, and figure Dan and I'd better stick together. I hide behind the front hall staircase with the toe of my sneaker sticking out so he'll find me right away. Then the two of us go through the house looking for Richie and John. It takes a long time to find them, and it's scary to open a door and not know what will be on the other side.

We finally find John hiding under a sheet in a bathtub on the second floor, and Richie in a closet on the third floor. Dan thinks Richie was real brave to stay alone in a dark closet for all the time that it took us to find him. But I think he hung out in the room until he heard us coming and then he went in the closet.

After that we lie on the floor in the living room facing the back lawn. I watch the leaves falling off the trees and look for birds. "I wonder what it would be like to live here?" I ask out loud. "You know, if you were real rich and could afford it and everything. What would you do if you had this whole place to yourself?"

"First of all, I wouldn't be alone," John says. "I'd fill it with beautiful women. And I'd get me the best sound system in the world, with music piped in every room. And I'd have at least five VCRs and TVs. And a swimming pool. Definitely a swimming pool."

"Me, too," Richie says. "And lots of servants."

"I'd put movie equipment in here," Dan says. "Not to just watch movies, but to make them. I'd get the best machines for doing special effects. Then I'd make monster films. Or just do the special effects for other people's films. Man, that'd be great."

"What about you?" John asks me.

I know exactly what I'd do, but I don't feel like telling John, so I say, "Nothing special. Just live here and have fun." But, I'm thinking, first I'd study to be a scientist who knows all about birds, an ornithologist. Then I'd turn the whole estate into a bird sanctuary and invite other ornithologists to do research with me. We'd take pictures and write about the birds. And I'd invite my grandpa Al to live here, too. He could grow vegetables and take care of the orchard and build things with me. He'd love that. If my father wanted to come over, I'd let him, but the minute he was mean to someone or embarrassed me, I'd send him away. Tyson could live with us if he wanted. So could my mother. And maybe Hilary. But they'd probably want to stay home with my father. I guess Grandpa and I would visit them. But anytime I wanted, I'd know I could walk out of their house, get in my big van, and drive home to my bird sanctuary.

Thursday night I study for my social studies test again. On the way to school I review the causes of the Revolutionary War. I finally know them all.

I get to the classroom just as the bell is ringing. Richie, Dan, and John are already in their seats. John gives me a big high five and grins as I pass him. "Brian, my man," he says.

Before I have a chance to sit down, Mr. Bigham says, "Brian, could I have your absentee note, please. Yours, too, Dan."

"For what?" I ask.

"What note, sir?" Dan asks.

"Your absentee notes for missing school yesterday," Mr. Bigham says.

"But there wasn't any school," I tell Mr. Bigham, "because of the furnace. It was on the radio."

"It was too dangerous to be here," Dan adds.

The whole class is hooting with laughter. Especially John and Richie, who are also scratching their heads. Isabel is laughing so hard that she doesn't even notice that they're doing it.

Mr. Bigham asks, "Boys, did you hear that school was closed on the radio, or did someone tell you?"

"Someone told us," I say. "Told us that they heard it on the radio."

"Who?" Mr. Bigham asks.

Dan and I exchange a glance that means we're not going to squeal on John and Richie, though I'm not quite sure why.

"Some guys on bikes," I tell Mr. Bigham.

When I sit down, Isabel whispers to me, "An emergency with the furnace in October? You couldn't make up anything better than that?" I feel like scratching my head and under my arms, too, right in her face. But I won't give John the satisfaction. If I scratch, he'll think I think what he did is funny. It isn't. Not one bit.

"It certainly is suspicious that all of four of you were absent on the same day," Mr. Bigham comments. "John's father called the school about his aunt's funeral, and I have Richie's note about his cold."

Richie fakes a sneeze and cough.

"But," Mr. Bigham continues, "you two don't have any real excuse, do you?"

"No, sir," Dan and I answer in unison.

Mr. Bigham doesn't make us say who told us that

there wasn't any school, but he's going to call our parents. I figure that Mr. Bigham is smart enough to know that John and Richie made up their excuse, and he'll call their parents, too. So I tell John that during lunch. I also ask him why he played such a mean trick on us.

"Who cares if Bigham calls my mother?" he says. "What's she going to do about it? And it was not a mean thing to do. I did it for your own good. You're getting too serious about school. You're getting too serious about everything. I figured you needed the day off to get back your Jokers Club attitude. Lighten up, man."

"What's the big deal?" Richie asks. "We cut all the time last year."

"I only cut three times," I tell him. "That's why my father's so strict with me this year. I'm going to get in big trouble because of cutting yesterday."

"Me, too," Dan says. "Big trouble."

"Everybody in the class got a good laugh out of it," John says. "And you had fun yesterday, admit it."

"Not enough fun to make up for what my father's going to do to me." I don't tell them I'm also worried that Mr. Dithers won't let me make up the social studies test. That after all the studying I've done, he'll give me a failing grade because I cut.

I'm about to bite into the cafeteria's version of individual pizza pie when the guys at the eighth-grade table call over to me, "Hey, Brian, there's no school Monday. They have to sweep the cafeteria." This gets a good laugh from the sixth- and seventh-grade tables.

I yell back, "Here's something for them to sweep up," and throw my pizza at them Frisbee-style. It hits Mac on the sleeve, sauce side up, before dropping to the floor. Everyone in the cafeteria is cheering and laughing. Richie, John, and Dan scratch. So Isabel throws her pizza at them, making a bull's-eye on the back of Richie's head.

I get the Joker points for the day, and Isabel and I get lunchroom detention for all of the next week.

9

Isabel: 2 Points
+ 1 Big Joke Point

There are two parts to lunchroom detention. First, instead of eating with your friends in the cafeteria, you eat your lunch at a kid's-sized table in the corner of the kitchen. Second, when your class goes out to the schoolyard, you stay inside to help the staff clean up for the next lunch period. Ms. Freedman says that when we see how hard the kitchen staff works, we'll have more respect for cafeteria rules like "No throwing food." I've never had lunchroom detention before.

"I've never had any detentions," Isabel tells me as we sit down at the little table with our lunches. I move the blue plastic fork through the orange macaroni and cheese goo. Isabel opens the lunch she brought from home. I watch her take a bite of a delicious-looking ham-and-cheese sandwich. A big frosted brownie is peeking out of her lunch bag.

"How many detentions have you had?" she asks.

"Enough," I tell her.

She takes another bite of that sandwich. There are bright red tomato slices in it. And lots of mayonnaise.

One of the cafeteria workers comes over to give us each an extra milk. "My, my," he says to Isabel, "I never thought I'd see a good girl like you eating her lunch back here."

"Some boys were making fun of me," she says. "I had to defend myself." She sits up straighter, like she's proud of herself, and says, "You can't let people push you around."

"*YOU* threw food?" he says.

"I'm sorry," she says.

I tell him I'm sorry, too.

While we're eating, I think about the Jokers Club and Operation J.D.B.R. It doesn't feel like we're much of a club anymore. Not with John making jokes on me and tricking Dan and me into cutting school. And if Isabel, who sits right next to me, is going to go into a screaming, foot-stamping, food-throwing rage every time I scratch my head for the Jokers Club, we'll both be in trouble all year. So I tell her, "That whole scratching thing, that the guys do. They're not doing it to make fun of you." I explain about the Jokers Club and how scratching is a sign that a joke is good. That it's not about her.

"It may not have started out to be about me," she says. "But it is now. They look right at me when they scratch."

"Not me," I tell her. "I'd never do that."

"And what about my nickname, Is-a-ape?"

"How'd you know about that?" I ask. I'm feeling sorry about making up that mean name for her.

"One of you guys wrote it in yellow chalk on my book bag," she says as she takes the brownie out of her lunch bag.

"Not me," I tell her. "Dan wouldn't, either."

"It was probably John," she says. "Whenever I walk by him, he whispers, 'Is-a-ape.' Next time he does that, I'm going to do something violent. And those prissy, silly girls — Charlene, Beth, and Mona. I'm not taking any more of their nonsense, either. The next time one of them makes fun of the way I dress or says that I'm fat" — she makes a fist and throws it in the air — "Pow, right in the kisser."

I'm super-shocked. I picture her turning into this troublemaker who dresses only in black leather, has a dozen tattoos, and beats up on everyone with brass knuckles.

I tell her, "You've always been the best kid in the class. You get the highest grades, and you're a real teacher's pet." She glares at me. "But being a teacher's pet isn't your fault," I continue. "Teachers naturally like you because you're so smart."

She unwraps the brownie and licks the frosting off her fingers. My mouth waters.

"You don't understand," she says. "I'm sick of being a good girl. None of you respect me because

I'm smart. Well, maybe you'll respect me when I'm tough."

She eats the brownie and washes it down with her extra milk. "I'm going to lift weights for strength," she says between bites and slurps. "I think I'll take boxing lessons, too."

I think maybe Isabel has totally lost her mind.

After the kids clear out of the cafeteria, we help two of the kitchen staff clean up while the first five grades file in for their lunch period. There are spills and sticky ketchup blobs to mop up, containers to throw in the trash, books left behind to put on the lost-and-found shelf. It's amazing what slobs some kids are.

After school, I'm so busy telling Mrs. Samuels that I'm grounded for two weekends because of cutting school and that I got lunchroom detention for throwing pizza that I don't even notice the portable computer on the desk in front of us.

When I ask her whose it is, she flips the screen open and explains, "The school system presented this laptop computer to me when I retired. It's better than a watch and a plaque like they gave Mr. Anderson, don't you think?"

I agree, then ask, "Am I going to use it?"

"Yes, indeed. And we'll get you into the school's computer room, too."

The first thing I learn to do on her computer is

open my own work disk and make a header. Then she types in some words broken into syllables. I read the words by syllables and tell which rule each syllable follows. Next I learn how to bring the syllables together on the computer screen and read them out loud again. Then she tests me on the spelling words she gave me for homework, and I try out some new words. We don't cover as many words as usual, but she says that's because I don't know where the letters are on the keyboard.

After we turn off the computer, she says, "I have an idea for this lunchroom detention of yours. We're going to put it to good use. I'll arrange for you to work in the computer room. As soon as you've eaten your lunch tomorrow, meet me there and I'll show you how to use this book." She holds up a book that teaches typing. "By Friday you'll be able to type without looking at the keyboard."

I don't believe I can learn to type in four days, but she says the lessons in the book will teach me in a much better way than the way they taught typing when she went to school.

I walk her to her car so I can carry the computer. She says I'm a gentleman, but I know that the real reason I'm carrying the computer is because I'm pretending it's mine.

When we get to the car, she takes the computer from me, puts it on the seat of her car, and asks, "How's your father doing?"

"You know my dad?" I ask back.

"I certainly do," she says. "I was Roy Toomey's second-grade teacher. I taught him how to read, too."

"Was he dyslexic?"

"Probably," she says. "We didn't have a name for it then. But I was thinking about Roy Toomey just the other day, and I'd say yes, he is dyslexic. He had a hard time learning to read, just like you."

"He's not a very good speller," I tell her.

"Learning differences, like dyslexia, are often inherited. Especially from father to son."

I tell her about the postcard we got from my grandpa Al and that he's my father's father. We agree he's probably dyslexic, too. Then I ask her, "Did my father have a tutor?"

"No. I was his regular teacher. The way we taught reading in those days, sooner or later everybody seemed to catch on. Maybe not in first grade. But if a child like your father couldn't read when they came through the door of my second-grade classroom, I knew I had my work cut out for me. I'd try different teaching methods until I hit on something that worked with him. I probably did the same things with your father that I'm doing with you."

"But not on a computer."

"No. Not on a computer."

I watch the way her smile connects up all the wrinkles on her face, which makes me smile, too. "Just remember," she says, "it's the teacher that counts, not the computer. No computer can replace Mrs. Samuels."

I know she's right. But someday I won't have Mrs. Samuels. That's when I hope I have a computer just like the one in the front seat of her car. As I'm walking across the schoolyard, I think about how my grandpa is still a terrible speller and what my mother said about the Valentine's Day card my father sent her. I decide that if I ever send a Valentine's Day card to a girl, which I doubt I ever will, I won't write anything but my name.

I'm on my bike before I see what's printed in big yellow chalk on the pavement next to the bike rack. BRAIN AND IS-A-APE. I have no trouble reading it or figuring out who wrote it.

I take off my jacket and use it to rub the pavement clean.

When I get home I call Dan and tell him that no way am I friends with John anymore. As far as I'm concerned, there is no club. "And if you value your life," I tell him, "don't scratch when John or Richie make a joke because Isabel is turning mean and dangerous."

"Our Is-a-ape?"

"I wouldn't call her that if I were you," is my parting advice to him.

The next day I don't wait for John to ride bikes to school with me. When he comes into the class-room making some stupid joke about a bad smell in the room, I don't pay any attention to him. But I do pay attention when Isabel comes in. Every-body does. For a second I'm not even sure it is Isabel.

Her black hair isn't long and bushy and hanging in her face anymore. It's cut short — very short — and slicked back away from her face. She's not wear-ing a baggy skirt and sweater like the old Isabel, but black jeans, cowboy boots, and a red T-shirt. Instead of holding her books in a high pile in front of her chest, she has a bright yellow backpack slung over her shoulder. She doesn't look as fat as I thought she was. Her body's just more developed than the other girls.

Charlene, who sits in front of me, leans over and whispers to Beth, "Is that really Isabel?" and Beth answers, "What a make-over!"

Mr. Bigham says, "Good morning, Isabel. I like your new haircut."

She says, "Thank you," and heads up the aisle to her seat. John, like always, is tipped back in his chair. He mumbles, "You're still Is-a-ape," as she passes him. In an instant, John — and his chair — are on the floor.

A lot of kids laugh, including me.

"What happened there, John?" Mr. Bigham asks.

"Nothing," John says as he rights himself.

Isabel sits down. She's got a defiant don't-mess-with-me look, but I notice that her hands are shaking when she unzips her backpack to take out her books. I wonder if now that she's tough-looking she'll stop being smart in school. But she asks and answers as many questions as ever. She just looks different. I decide she's used some of her smarts to figure out how to dress and act if you don't want other kids to make fun of you.

During our morning classes Isabel gets three notes from other girls. When we sit down together for our lunchroom detention, I ask her, "What were all those notes about?"

"They all wanted to know the same thing, who cut my hair."

I wonder if Isabel was hoping some of those girls would finally ask her to be their friend.

"Who did cut it?" I ask.

"My grandfather. He's a barber. He didn't want me to have it cut off, but he said if anyone was going to cut my hair, he should." I imagine Isabel and her grandpa in the barbershop with all that wavy black hair on the floor. I wonder how her mother and father feel about her haircut and new way of dressing.

Then she asks me if I know where she can take boxing lessons. I tell her what I've learned about self-defense and being tough from karate.

"Not for me," she says. "I want to lift weights and box."

After we finish eating I finally get up my courage to tell Isabel that I won't be cleaning the cafeteria with her. That Mrs. Samuels got permission for me to use my lunchroom detention to work in the computer room. I explain that because of my dyslexia, I need to learn how to type.

She's glaring at me. "You mean I have to clean the cafeteria, and you get to use a computer?" she says.

"Yeah, I guess."

"No fair. We both threw pizza. If your so-called punishment is to learn how to type on a computer, it should be my punishment, too." She slaps her hand on the table. "I'm coming with you."

We leave the cafeteria kitchen by the back way. I tell Isabel it's a short cut, but it's also the only way to get out of there without everyone in the sixth, seventh, and eighth grade seeing me with Isabel-as-Wonder Woman.

Friday during journal writing, I write the whole time.

Im learning how to tipe. It is fun. I can tipe with out loking at the keys. I spel beater to. When I get up to a beater spelling level I can use spell cheak and correct all my speling on the computer. John and richey dont like me to much becuse I don't horse around in school so mush. there geting all the jocker points this week for jocks that arent so funny. dan is still my frend. After we got in big troubl for missing schol his mouther and father came to school. Now dan is doing all his work in school. Everyone in awer class was surprized that dan is smart. I think he's even smarter than isabel. dan would never need a tuter. He was not doing well in school becouse he thought richey and John and me would not be his freand if he was good in school. Now he knows I like him smart. So do a lot of kids. I wish I were writing this on the computer. I like to tipe. I hate to wright.

95

I have to go straight home after school to start my first weekend of being grounded and to baby-sit for Tyson while my mother goes grocery shopping. He and I start out in his room because that's where most of his toys are. He hands me a tub of Play-doh and commands, "Make animals." We sit cross-legged on the floor while I make him a yellow cow, a yellow horse, and a yellow duck — all about three inches high. I line them up on the floor. "Let's play with them," I tell him. "You can be the farmer."

"More," he says. He waddles across his room, digs out two more tubs of Play-doh from the bottom of his toy box, waddles back, and drops them in my lap. "More animals."

"Okay," I tell him. "But you have to help." I show him how to roll the Play-doh into little blue eyes. That keeps him busy while I make a red sheep, a red dog, a red cat, and a red rooster. I help him stick the eyes on and then I cut barn doors in an empty shoe box and make a silo out of the cardboard center of a toilet paper roll.

"Brian," my mother yells up the stairs, "get down here and unload the car."

"I'll tell you a story about the animals before you go to sleep tonight," I tell Tyson. "How's that?"

Tyson holds up the cow. "Make a car. Make a car," he demands.

"I made you all those animals," I say.

He squinches up his face to start crying and squishes up the cow to destroy it.

"Hey," I yell. "Quit it."

Too late. He's stamped on the duck and the cat and is mauling the sheep with his free hand. "Cars. Make cars," he cries.

I hate seeing my animals demolished. Sometimes Tyson really gets me mad.

"Brian, did you hear me?" my mother shouts.

"I hear you," I yell back. "I hear you."

I leave Tyson crying over his Play-doh corpses and run downstairs.

As I'm lifting the first bag of groceries out of the back of the car, my dad's pickup pulls into the driveway. Miracle of miracles, he comes over to help me.

"Aren't you supposed to be with your tutor now?" he asks.

"Not on Friday," I answer. "She said she was your second-grade teacher. Her name is Mrs. Samuels."

He piles a second bag in my arms and picks up two bags himself. "I don't remember her," he says. "Who remembers second grade?"

"She says you didn't know how to read when you got to her class. That she taught you how."

We head toward the back door with our loads. "Well," he says, "somebody must have taught me."

I think it's pretty amazing that my dad can't remember the one person who taught him how to read, when Mrs. Samuels, with all the hundreds of kids she taught to read, remembers him.

We're putting down the bags. "Oh, yeah," he says. "I remember Mrs. Samuels. She was real strict. She used to keep me after school. All my friends would go off to play, and I had to stay in and review with these flash cards. But she'd give me a snack first. Banana bread and juice." He's actually smiling.

"She gives me banana bread, too," I tell him. "Same thing. She must really love banana bread. I'll tell her that you remember."

"Sure," he says. "Why not?" Tyson's coming down the stairs, crying his head off. "Why's your brother crying?" my dad asks me. His smile has turned into a glare. "I thought you were supposed to be taking care of him."

By the time dinner's ready, I've turned Tyson's mangled duck into a race car, his sheep into a pickup truck, his horse into a backhoe, the cow into a van, the cat and rooster into a dump truck, the shoe box barn into a garage. With scissors and tape I turn the toilet paper roll silo into three gas pumps.

Saturday. I'm grounded for cutting school. I do a lot of thinking.

Sunday. I'm still grounded. I do some more thinking.

Monday morning I wait on my bike for John to come by. Before I can tell him what I've been thinking about all weekend, he says to me, "Brian, my man, you didn't put your two bucks into the Operation J.D.B.R. pot last week. You or Dan. You'd better cough it up today." He pedals on down the street.

I pull up alongside him and say. "Listen, John, after what you did to Dan and me, I figure Operation J.D.B.R. is over. I want the money back that I put in already."

He laughs. "You're kidding, right? We don't split the pot until Christmas, remember?"

I try to keep my voice from quivering when I say, "Dan and I are half the club, and we say the Operation is over. We want our money back."

"Look," John says, "you two agreed to something and you better stick to it or you'll have more trouble than you could ever imagine."

"For us, it's over," I say. "And you have our money."

"You keep paying two dollars a week," he says. "And at the end, we divide it up by points." A car honks to pass, so I have to drop behind John. He yells over his shoulder, "Tell that wimp Dan, too." I take my time riding the rest of the way to school.

Dan is waiting for me at the bike rack. We walk the longest way possible to our classroom so we have time to talk without bumping into Richie or John.

I tell Dan that John says we can't drop out of Operation J.D.B.R.

"But I've got to quit joking and fooling around so much in school," he says. "I'm getting too much grief from my parents. If we're putting money into the pot without making Joker points, it's like giving it away to them."

"We haven't even been laughing at their stupid jokes, and they say they're making points," I say. "If it keeps going on like this, they'll win most of the money."

Dan takes only a second to figure out how much money is involved. "At $32 each, the pot will be worth $128 by Christmas. But you and I will lose most of our investment."

"This is a bad situation," I say.

We agree that we've got to tell John and Richie that we aren't members of the Jokers Club anymore, and that we want our money back from Operation J.D.B.R.

"Easy to say. Hard to do," Dan says. "Remember, they're bigger than we are."

"And meaner," I remind him.

"But we're smarter," he reminds me.

"And," I add, "we're on the side of right."

Isabel comes striding down the hall with her new no-nonsense tough attitude. "Hey, Brian," she says as she passes, "how's it going?"

"Good," I tell her, even though for me, things don't seem to be going good at all.

"Hey, Danny," she says, "I can press thirty-five pounds. How about you?"

"Ah. Yeah, way to go, Isabel," he calls after her. He turns to me and says, "Weights?"

I shrug my shoulders and say, "I told you so."

"So what are we going to do?" Dan asks as we walk the last stretch of hall to our classroom.

"Maybe we should go along with them a little longer while we figure out how we can get out of the club without losing our money."

"Or getting beaten to a bloody pulp," Dan adds.

At lunch, Dan and I fork over our two dollars to John, and Dan records the Operation J.D.B.R. scores for the week. John, 12 points; Richie, 8 points; Brian, 2, Dan, 0.

10

John: 2 Points
+ 1 Big Joke Point

When we've split into our animal groups on Thursday, Mr. Bigham says, "Class, your animal reports are due next week. If you haven't done it yet, now is the time to think of an original way to present what you've learned about your animal to the rest of us."

Isabel and I look at one another. A moment of panic flashes over her face. "Uh-oh," she says. "All we've got are my notes and a tape recording that everybody's already heard."

"Look at John," Richie calls out.

I hear John before I see him. He's making a loud noise through his nose that sounds more like a pig snorting than a person snoring. But snoring is what he means by it, because he's lying across two desks, pretending to be asleep. Mr. Bigham goes over and talks to him in a low voice.

"But, Mr. Bigham," John says in a voice loud enough for everyone to hear, "I am doing my work.

This is part of my animal project. Hibernation."

Everyone, except Mr. Bigham, is laughing. "What a nut case," Isabel says. When she's not looking, I give a quick scratch to my head. John sees it and smirks at me.

"Enough," Mr. Bigham says.

We all go back to work, and John gets back in his seat.

Isabel and I review her notes. I learn that the average Canada goose lives for twenty years and that they mate for life. I also find out that I was right about their honking sound being a way of communicating. The male makes a two-syllable A-HONK sound. The female answers with a higher pitched, single-syllable HINK call. And when they're defending their territory, they make a HISS call.

"This is all great stuff," I tell her. "You have to tell the class everything you told me."

"You should play your tape," she says, "so they can hear the way the Canada goose honks. And what you said on the tape was great, just like a real reporter."

I tell her I wish I'd known more about the Canada goose when I made the tape. That instead of saying I'm surprised at how big the geese look when they fly close to me, I'd say that the average length of a Canada goose is three and one half feet, and the wingspan is five and one half feet, which is as tall as I am. "And," I add, "when I describe where they're eating, I could have said that they mostly feed in the early morning and at sunset, but that they also feed throughout the day, especially when they're in family groups. Just like you told me."

"I wish I could've seen it all like you did," she says.

"I wish we could show everyone in the class what I saw," I tell her. That's when I get a brilliant idea. "Let's make a videotape. We can do our whole report in front of a camera. And we'll videotape the geese feeding."

"A nature film," Isabel says. "Why not?"

"Because I don't have a video camera."

"Neither do I."

"But Dan's father does," I tell her. "And Dan loves to make home movies. He'll be our cameraperson."

By the time the bell rings, we've each selected the topics we'll talk about on our nature video, "A Close Look at the Canada Goose." After my tutoring session, Mrs. Samuels and I use the computer to write an outline of my speech. We print it out in the computer room.

Saturday afternoon Dan and Tyson and I wait on my steps for Isabel. "You sure she can ride a bike?" Dan asks. "I've never seen her on one."

"I told her we needed to move fast, and she said she had wheels."

Just then we see big Isabel pedaling down my block. She's wearing a tough-looking black leather jacket, but is all humped over this little kid's violet-and-pink bike, huffing and puffing just to get the tiny wheels to carry her weight.

Dan and I look at one another. No way can Isabel keep up with us on that bike.

"Is that your bike?" I ask when she gets off.

"My sister's," she says.

"How old is your sister?" Dan asks.

"Seven." As she takes her loaded backpack off her shoulders, she looks us right in the eye. We know better than to joke about the bike.

Before we go looking for geese, Dan says we should practice talking in front of the camera. We rehearse in the backyard. Then we go inside so he can shoot the title cards and photos of Canada geese in the books that Isabel borrowed from the library. Tyson follows us everywhere and manages to put himself in every shot.

We play back the rehearsal and titles on the television set. He loves it. "Tyson on TV," he shouts. "Tyson on TV."

When Hilary comes in from soccer practice, I introduce her to Isabel and show her the terrific camera that Dan's using. But Hilary's more interested in Isabel. "Nice haircut," my sister says. "Where'd you get it?"

"My grandfather's a barber," Isabel explains. "He'd cut your hair, too, if you want."

They get into an intense conversation about hairstyles that I interrupt to ask, "Hilary, can Isabel borrow your bike and helmet, just for this afternoon?" She agrees, and half an hour later the three of us are headed for the Colgate mansion. Dan with the camera bag over his shoulder. Me and Isabel with the scripts and snacks in our backpacks.

As we approach the field through the woods, Dan and I exchange a worried look. What if John and Richie are there with the eighth graders? Or what if they come while we're in the gardener's shed trying to make our movie?

After we hide our bikes in a new place, I check through the window that no one's in the shed. Then I signal Dan and Isabel that it's all clear.

"So this is where the fearsome four hang out," Isabel comments as she follows us into the shed. "Big deal."

I ignore her and plop down on my old haystack. I'm remembering all the fun we had over the summer and feel sad. "I'm not coming back here anymore," I tell her.

"Me, either," Dan says from his sandbag chair.

There's a low mood in the shed until Isabel shouts, "Hey, aren't we here to make a movie?"

I direct Isabel to stand in the middle of the field

and explain the migration patterns of the Canada goose. Dan tapes it.

Isabel says I should stand next to the pond beyond the field while I describe the mating and nesting habits of the Canada goose. Because part of my brain is thinking about all the jokes John will make when he sees the tape, I'm nervous and make lots of mistakes. The second time I get through it without stammers and nervous laughs.

Then Dan directs Isabel to sit on the front step of the shed for her next part, which is about the way the early settlers used the geese for meat and their feathers for bed stuffing. I join her there to explain that Canada geese eat bulbs, berries, roots, and post-harvest grains — which is why we're at this location.

We turn off the camera and go back into the shed and wait for the geese to come feed in the field. I notice our backpacks that hold the food Isabel brought. "Talk about eating," I say, "let's do it."

While Dan props the camera in the window facing the field, Isabel and I unpack cartons of milk and Isabel-style sandwiches and brownies. After we eat, we sit back and wait for the geese. Dan and I tell Isabel about the eighth graders that John and Richie have been bringing to the hideout, about the gun, about how we don't want to be in a club with them anymore, and about the money under the shed. "I think we should just take out our share of the money, right now," I tell Dan. "It's ours."

"So they can come and kill us when they find it missing?" he says.

Isabel gets on our case about being afraid of John and Richie. "They don't even care about you guys," she says. "They're too busy trying to impress those eighth-grade jerks with what big shots they are. I can't believe that your money is right here, under this shed, and you're not taking it."

"I value my life," I tell her.

In the distance we hear "A-HONK. HINK. A-HONK. HINK." Dan, who's already at his post by the window, videotapes the geese's approach. I stand next to him and begin my voice-over describing the way Canada geese fly in loose flocks when going short distances, and in a V-formation for longer trips. "These geese," I note, "are in a loose grouping. But," I add disappointedly, "they are flying right over our field and off toward New York State. They won't be stopping here for dinner."

Dan turns off the camera, and I turn to Isabel and ask, "Why didn't they stop? Don't they usually come back to the same places?"

"Not when guns have been shot at them," she says. "You should have told me about that before and I would have said they'd never come back here. Canada geese are smart. They don't want to hang around John and Richie, either."

I watch the flock of geese — black specks disappearing into the scarlet sunset sky. "We'd never catch up with them," I say. "On any kind of bike."

"I've got to get home, anyway," Dan comments as he starts packing up the camera.

"Wait here a minute," Isabel says. "I have to go outside." I figure she's going to go pee in the woods, just like a guy has to sometimes.

I don't find out what Isabel was really doing out there until the next day.

11

The End of
the Jokers Club

In our house Tyson is the first one to wake up. On Sundays, when he sees that my parents are still sleeping, he climbs the attic stairs to get me up. But this Sunday I'm already awake and dressed. I bring him back down to my parents' room and rub my mother's arm to wake her up. "Mom," I say. "I gotta go out. Here's Tyson."

She squints up at me for a second, closes her eyes again, and puts the blanket over her head. "Go away," she mumbles from under the covers.

"Dad," I say in a louder voice. "Take care of Tyson."

My father sits up on his elbow. "It's six in the morning. You take care of Tyson."

"I have to go look for geese. For school. I told you last night. It's homework."

His voice is groggy, but his tone is stern. "Brian, you're taking care of Tyson. We're sleeping. Look

for your geese later on. They're not going anywhere."

"You can't find them so much unless they're eating," I tell him. "They eat early."

He's not listening. He's back under the covers,
too.

"Me go look for goose birds," Tyson says. "Me
go."

I take Tyson to Hilary's room. Waking Hilary on
a Sunday morning is harder than convincing a sleepy
old volcano it should erupt. And if you do manage
to wake her up, she's as fiery as a volcano. I think
about this as I'm going into her room, turn around,
and leave.

"Go look for birds," Tyson insists.

I put on his jacket and take him outside where
Dan and Isabel are already waiting for me. The half-
moon is still bright over our house. While Isabel
takes Hilary's bike out of the garage, I get out my
mother's bike and stick Tyson in his seat. We put
on our helmets and we're off.

"Good morning, moon," Tyson chants. "Good
morning, sky." He keeps it up as we pedal down
the street. "Good morning, bike. Good morning,
birds. Good morning, goose birds."

"Tyson's okay," Dan tells me.

Isabel is leading us to a farm field that she's convinced will be a breakfast spot for Canada geese. As
we bike along dirt roads, we watch the sun — a

watermelon-pink sphere — rising over blue-gray hills. After a couple of miles we come to the field. We find a hiding place for ourselves in the bushes.

The first animals to come are deer that feed on the old cornstalks. We count thirteen of them. Dan tapes that for our movie. Next he tapes two squirrels chasing one another around and up a big tree.

"Good morning, goose birds! Good morning, goose birds!" Tyson is pointing at the sky beyond the field and we all hear the perfect soundtrack for our nature film. A-HONK. HINK. A-HONK. HINK. Dan keeps the tape rolling as about one hundred Canada geese land in the field. We watch them eat, and Dan zooms in on a goose who's standing guard.

After a minute or so I whisper to Isabel, "Follow me. I have an idea." I tell Dan to hold his post and to keep taping no matter what happens.

Isabel and Tyson and I creep behind the bushes that surround the field. When we're on the opposite side, we slowly walk into the field. A sentinel goose sees us, warns the others with a HISS call. In an instant the flock is up in the air, honking as they fly right toward and over Dan.

"Good-bye, goose," my brilliant little brother calls out. Dan slowly lowers the camera and zooms in on Tyson, who's waving up toward the sky and shouting, "Bye-bye, goose. So long. See you later."

We sit on a rock and take turns watching the playback in the viewfinder. We congratulate each other and Tyson on a great video. But Tyson doesn't care. He's screwing up his face in a grimace and pulling on my hand. "Juice, juice," he whimpers.

"Let's all go to my house," Dan says. "My dad'll make us breakfast, and we can watch the tape."

"Me, too?" Isabel asks.

"Sure," Dan says, "why not?"

"His father makes awesome pancakes," I tell her.

While Dan's father is cooking and Tyson is slurping down a second glass of juice, Isabel motions us to follow her into the living room. "Here's your money, guys," she says as she hands us each an envelope.

I look in the envelope and count one five and five singles. Ten dollars.

Dan holds up the stack of bills that are in his envelope. "You got this from John?" he asks her.

"Sort of," she says.

I picture Isabel holding John in a wrestler's arm lock, demanding he give us back our money. "How?" I ask.

"Look, it's your money. Now you have it."

Dan's got it figured out. "You took it from under the shed yesterday. When you said you had to go outside."

She nods.

"They'll know we took it," I say.

"You didn't take it," she says. "I took it. And I'm not afraid of those bozos."

"Breakfast is ready," Dan's father calls.

We don't talk about the money again until we've brought Hilary's bike and Tyson back to my house. That whole time I'm thinking about Isabel and the money. The last thing I want is for the kids at school to think that Isabel is like my bodyguard, taking care of my problems with John. It's a ridiculous situation and will make Dan and me the subject of about ten thousand jokes.

As Isabel is rolling out her sister's bike to ride on home, I tell her, "Isabel, I'm not going to let you take the rap for getting us our money."

"Me, either," Dan says.

She gets on the bike. "It's okay," she says. "I told you I'm not afraid of those guys." She rides off down the street on the little pink-and-violet bike.

"We aren't, either," Dan calls after her.

"We should write them a letter," I tell Dan, "and leave it under the shed. Let's be totally up front about it."

Dan agrees, so we sit on the steps and compose this letter.

Dear John and Richie,

We the undersigned, Dan and Brian, do not want to be in a club with you anymore. The Jokers Club is different now, for two reasons:

#1. *You brought other people in without discussing it with us.*

#2. *You broke rule #2 of Operation J.D.B.R. when you turned the jokes against a club member, Brian, and said you should get points for that.*

Since we've quit the Jokers Club and, as far as we're concerned, Operation J.D.B.R. is over, we have to decide what to do with the stash of cash. If we divide the money by points, ending with the time that you, John, started making jokes on Brian, we would have earned much more than half the pot. But we decided to just take what we put into it. Five weeks at two dollars a week equals ten dollars apiece.

Just because we aren't in the club with you anymore doesn't mean that we should be enemies. We can still be friends — kind of — just not in a club together.

Sincerely yours,

Brian A. Toomey and Daniel R. Chester

P.S. There was only $23 in the pot, even though there should have been $40. Sorry, Richie, but we took what was ours.

* * *

"Are you scared?" I ask Dan as we sneak through the woods toward the hideout.

"Yup," he answers. "But not as afraid as I'm going to be when John and Richie read this." He pulls the letter out of his pocket. "Let's get it over with."

We run the rest of the way. Just as we've stuck the folded letter next to the remaining stash of cash in the tobacco tin, a gunshot BANG! goes off on the roof of the mansion. We don't look up to see who fired it. We don't stop to hear what John is shouting at us. We do get out of there as fast as is humanly possible — which is pretty fast.

"Well, Brian," my father says at dinner that night, "did you get that American history test back yet?"

I nod.

"So, how'd you do?" my mother asks.

"Okay." I look at the mound of mashed potatoes and the fried chicken leg on my plate. With a sinking feeling in my empty stomach, I realize that I'm not going to enjoy my dinner.

"What's 'okay'?" my father persists. "What was your grade? An A, I hope."

"I got a C," I mumble.

"I thought you were supposed to be smart," Hilary says.

"Don't pick on him," my mother scolds.

"How come?" my father asks me. "Didn't you

study enough? Another C and it's good-bye karate lessons, young man."

"Yes, sir," I answer.

I don't bother telling him that I studied more than I've ever studied for anything in my life. That Ms. Crandal helped me during resource period, and that Mr. Dithers let me take as long as I needed on the answers. I don't even tell him that Mr. Dithers wrote "very good" in the margin next to my essay answers. That I made all my mistakes on short answers like, "What year did the Revolutionary War end?" That I couldn't have remembered the answers to some memorization questions even if I'd stayed at my desk all day and night.

I flatten out my mashed potatoes with the fork.

"Don't be discouraged," my mother says. "You'll get over this dyslexia business. It'll just take time."

I look at her across the table and say, "I'll never get over it. Dad didn't. Neither did Grandpa Al."

"If you're not going to get over it, why are we bothering with all this tutoring?" my father asks.

I can't believe he says this. He's not "bothering" with anything. It doesn't even cost him any money. I'm the one who has to stay after school. I'm the one who has the extra homework. I'm the one who's beginning to wonder if it's worth it.

"Rain, rain, go away. Come again another day.

Little Tyson wants to play." Hilary is teaching the rhyme to Tyson as we're eating breakfast the next morning.

I love that it's raining. Rain means I won't be riding my bike, which means I won't have to see John until we're in school. "Dad," I ask, "can you give me a ride to school?"

"Okay," he says. "But I'm leaving right now. So put a move on."

A minute later I'm watching the wipers fan the rain back and forth across the windshield of the pickup and fantasizing about what John and Richie and their eighth-grade pals might do to me. How brave will I be, I wonder, if John says the ten dollars has to go back in the pot and I have to give him two dollars a week no matter what? Will they beat me up? Or put lit cigarettes out on my flesh? Maybe they'll threaten to shoot me. What if they say they'll hurt Tyson if I don't pay up?

My father glances sideways at me. "Why so low, Joe?" he asks.

"Nothing," I answer.

"Your mother says I discouraged you last night. About your schoolwork. I told her you are a tough kid and you can take it."

I shift nervously in my seat. Is it possible that my father is going to apologize to me for being such a bully?

"So can you take it?" he asks.

"Take what?"

"How hard life can get?" he says. "I only expect a lot from you because I know now that you can do it. So was I right?"

"I guess," I answer. "We'll see."

"Hey," my dad says, "here's that pal of yours." He swerves the truck over to the curb and comes to a stop. "Move over. We'll give him a ride."

I slide over to make room, but don't see which pal it is until the door opens and John gets in next to me.

"Thanks," he says to my dad.

"Nothing to it," my dad replies.

I keep my eyes on the windshield wipers and none of us says another word the rest of the way to school.

I hold my breath as John and I get out of the truck and start walking in the rain to the school entrance. But he still doesn't say anything. When he spots Mac, he gives me a little shove, says, "If you tell, man, you're dead," and moves off.

Mac is eyeing me suspiciously. Not like he's going to kill me, but like he's a little bit afraid of me. That's when I realize that Dan and I have something to hold over John and his new pals and maybe, just maybe, they won't be extinguishing red-hot cigarettes in our flesh. I run into the front hall to catch up to them. "Hey, John, Mac," I call out, "wait up."

They turn, arms folded on their chests, to face

me. "Yeah," Mac growls, "whaddaya want?"

I fold my arms over my chest, too. I'm scared, but I still say what's on my mind. "I'll forget what I saw you guys doing yesterday. I'll forget that you were fooling around with guns. But you forget all about Dan and me and don't give us any grief. None. Zippo. Not a bit."

"You're out of the club, man," John says. "You blew it."

"You pathetic little worm," Mac says. "Why would we want to have anything to do with you? You don't exist."

"Exactly," I say. "We don't exist."

I can't wait to tell Dan the good news.

Epilogue

Brian: 2 Points + 1 Big Point

It's a sunny June day. I look at the clock. Summer vacation starts in exactly one hour. I open my journal to write my last entry as a sixth grader. But I'm so excited about vacation starting that I can't think of anything to write about. As if he's read my mind again, Mr. Bigham says, "Listen up, class. If you're so excited about vacation starting that you you can't think of anything to write in your journal, why don't you write about your hopes and plans for the summer."

I pick up my pen and begin.

My plan for this summer is to make and sale bird houses with my grandfather. I hope we'll sale lots of them. We're going to study different birds and learne aboute the kinds of shilters they like. On weekends we're going to the crafes fars in the diffrent towns around here to sale them. We'll explane to are customars how to set them up so the birds they want to attract will us them. Grandpa says we'll pobly learn a lot about birds from are customers becaus lots of people love birds.

Another thing I'm going to do this summer is be tutered. Mrs. Samuels is going to come to my house ones a week to work with me. She's going to bring her computer. I'm going to be shore Grandpa Al is at are house sometimes when I have my vacation tutering. Mrs. Samuels is a widow. She isn't a rich widow, but she's a really nice one. I bet Grandpa Al will like her. Sens Mrs. Samuels likes me she's bound to like him.

I read over what I've written and think about my dyslexia. I know it's never going to go away. But it's not going to get worse, either. And I'm going to get better and better at the thinking things I am good at, like understanding birds, how things work, and having creative ideas.

I'm saving up to buy my own computer. In my journal I write the date and how much I've saved so far, $128.00. This is how I've saved so much money: I put away two dollars each week and my mother matches it with a two-dollar contribution. I decide that each time I sell a birdhouse, I'll write my share of the profits on this page and put the money away for my computer.

I close my journal and look around the room. A lot of other kids have stopped writing, too. Everyone's waiting for vacation to begin. But not Isabel. She's writing a mile a minute. She still gets on my nerves sometimes, which is a lot better than all the time. In a way, we're friends.

Charlene, George, Dan, and I taught her how to play basketball. She's tall and fast. She's stopped talking about boxing lessons, but I'll bet you anything she's still lifting weights.

I watch John. He's leaning back, balanced on the back legs of his chair, staring at the ceiling. He never writes in his journal. He doesn't make jokes anymore, either. A lot of days this year John didn't even come to school. Richie was in school more than

John, but he still didn't do much work. The Colgate mansion got sold to a drug rehabilitation center that's doing a big renovation. I don't know where John and Richie and their friends will hang out this summer. I don't really care.

Dan says I'm the most popular boy in our class now, but I think he is. I can see him writing in his journal now, or maybe he's drawing a new monster. When Dan started to wear glasses last month, John made a joke about it. Richie was the only one in our class who laughed.

Mr. Bigham stands up and announces, "Journal period is over and our year together is almost complete."

"About time," John mumbles.

If Mr. Bigham heard him, he pretends he didn't. But he certainly can hear him when John asks, "Can I be excused?"

"All right, John," Mr. Bigham answers. He holds out the big wooden boys' room pass, but John walks right by it and opens the door.

"So long, suckers," he shouts over his shoulder. With a slam of the door, he's gone for the year.

I can tell Mr. Bigham is disappointed that John never trusted him and that he couldn't help him with schoolwork. Mr. Bigham shakes his head and says, mostly to himself, "Now why'd he have to end the year like that?"

"Because he had to go," I call out.

Everyone in the room laughs, including Mr. Bigham.

Isabel and Dan scratch their heads.

Richie calls out, "Come on, Mr. Bigham, let us all go. There're only ten more minutes. The eighth grade's already out."

"Richie," he says, "stay right where you are. A few more minutes won't kill you. I have a present for you." Mr. Bigham opens up his desk drawer and takes out a pile of printed pamphlets.

Everyone's craning their necks and whispering, trying to figure out what it is. "It's probably a list of books we should read over the summer," Jenny says.

"I bet it's one of those things about not becoming a drug addict," Jason tells Isabel.

Isabel snickers. "You're wrong, Jason." I wonder, how come she knows what it is?

Mr. Bigham ends the suspense by telling us. "Isabel and I put together the poems that you wrote about your animal-life projects. Come up here, Isabel. Help pass them out."

Isabel strides up to the front of the room in her proud, tall way. Mr. Bigham hands her half of the pamphlets, and they each take a side of the room for handing them out.

Dan is one of the first to get his. He whistles

between his teeth. "This looks great," he says. "You got it printed and everything."

"We printed it ourselves," Isabel tells him. "With the school's desktop publishing program. I know how to do it now."

Mr. Bigham puts a pamphlet on my desk and pats me on the shoulder. "You had a good year, Brian," he says. "I'm proud of you."

I look down at the pamphlet. An ink drawing of a Canada goose, its wings outstretched, soars across the stiff sky-blue cover. It's a drawing that I did for art class. Dan's right. It does look great. Across the top I read, POEMS OF NATURE BY THE SIXTH-GRADE CLASS, SHARON CENTER SCHOOL. In the sky part, underneath the goose, all our names are printed in alphabetical order.

Everyone is flipping through the book to find their own poems. I find mine on page ten. "Canada Goose," by Brian Toomey.

"Shall we read some of them out loud?" Mr. Bigham asks.

Isabel calls out, "You do it, Mr. Bigham."

Everyone agrees. We know now that before Mr. Bigham was a teacher, he wasn't a criminal or a boxer. He was an actor. He still is. After we found that out, we were always begging him to take the parts when we studied plays in literature. One day, for fun, he took all the parts in the play *Our Town*. If you closed your eyes, you'd think there were a

126

whole bunch of people reading the roles instead of one sixth-grade teacher.

"Ready?" he says. We quiet down. He opens our book of poetry and begins. Some of the poems rhyme in a sing-songy way, but when Mr. Bigham says them, they sound good.

I think Dan's poem, "Raymond Comes to Dinner," is the best. It's a story-poem about a raccoon named Raymond who steals food from garbage cans. He has to be clever to outwit the neighbors who are trying to keep him from getting their garbage all over. In desperation, one guy keeps his garbage cans in his house. One night, as Raymond works his way from garbage can to garbage can, he's shocked to find nothing edible in any of them. Lucky for him, in the next stanza he figures what's happened to the garbage. The people on the street are putting their table scraps on compost heaps in their backyards. This is great for Raymond because he doesn't even have to figure out where the garbage cans are hidden or how to break into them. Each night he cruises the neighborhood backyards, going from compost heap to compost heap. The last stanza of the poem is:

> First course in the Smith's backyard.
> Dinner at the Bates'.
> The Jones' haven't finished yet.
> Dessert will have to wait.

* * *

Mr. Bigham says Dan's poem is a "Peter Rabbit" for the nineties.

When Mr. Bigham gets to my poem, he makes it sound so good, I can hardly believe I wrote it. He recites it in his deepest, most serious actor's voice. It's like he knows it by heart.

CANADA GOOSE

by Brian Toomey

Fly, Goose, fly free
So I can hear
The strength in your call.

Fly, Goose, fly free
So I can see
The power of your wings.

I cannot lean my body into wind
And move free through blue skies like you.

But, O great Canada goose, I can fly on
Wings of thought, soaring within my mindspace.

There I can be free and strong.

The bell rings. The school year is over.

About the Author

Jeanne Betancourt is also the author of many other Scholastic titles: the *Pony Pals* series (44 titles), *Ten True Animal Rescue Stories*, and the *Three Girls in the City* series (4 titles). Her books have been awarded several Children's Choice Awards. Jeanne's original teleplays have also received numerous awards, including six Emmy nominations, two Humanitas citations, and the National Psychological Award for Excellence in the Media. She received the 2004 Life Achievement Award from the Hamilton School at Wheeler.

Jeanne brings her own experience with dyslexia to this novel. She lives in New York City, where she draws, paints, writes, and tap dances. To learn more, check out her website at www.jeannebetancourt.com.

APPLE®PAPERBACKS

Pick an Apple and Polish Off Some Great Reading!

BEST-SELLING APPLE TITLES

❏ MT43944-8	**Afternoon of the Elves** Janet Taylor Lisle	**$3.99**
❏ MT41624-3	**The Captive** Joyce Hansen	**$3.50**
❏ MT43266-4	**Circle of Gold** Candy Dawson Boyd	**$3.99**
❏ MT44064-0	**Class President** Johanna Hurwitz	**$3.50**
❏ MT45436-6	**Cousins** Virginia Hamilton	**$3.99**
❏ MT43130-7	**The Forgotten Door** Alexander Key	**$3.99**
❏ MT44569-3	**Freedom Crossing** Margaret Goff Clark	**$3.99**
❏ MT42858-6	**The Hot and Cold Summer** Johanna Hurwitz	**$3.99**
❏ MT22514-2	**The House on Cherry Street 2: The Horror** Rodman Philbrick and Lynn Harnett	**$3.50**
❏ MT41708-8	**The Secret of NIMH** Robert C. O'Brien	**$4.50**
❏ MT42882-9	**Sixth Grade Sleepover** Eve Bunting	**$3.50**
❏ MT42537-4	**Snow Treasure** Marie McSwigan	**$3.99**

Available wherever you buy books, or use this order form